COUCH SURFING
THROUGH THE
12 CHAMBERS OF HELL

CURTIS M. LAWSON

COUCH SURFING
THROUGH THE
12 CHAMBERS OF HELL

ISBN: 978-1-957121-75-8

Text © 2024 by Curtis M. Lawson
Cover Artwork © 2024 by getcovers.com
Interior and cover design by César Puch

Editor and Publisher, Joe Morey

Weird House Press
Central Point, OR 97502
www.weirdhousepress.com

SEPTEMBER

"I have to warn you, Mr. Pharaoh, the photographs are ... gruesome." The man in the suit slides a tablet across the steel table. "Police and medical services weren't on site until nearly a full day after the event. Certain ... changes ... occur to the body in that time."

The body. What a terrible phrase. Say it aloud. Let it roll off your lips. Are there any two words so macabre when placed beside each other?

"Take your time," the suit adds. His voice is quiet and his tone respectful, but his eyes hold zero concern. "Just tap the screen when you're ready."

I take a deep breath and consider the black screen. It's a gateway of sorts—the threshold that separates dreams of hope and despair from indifferent reality. I touch the screen and it lights up revealing a gray corpse laid out on a table. Her face is puffy and discolored, but her features are a familiar work of art. The thin scar bisecting her right eyebrow. The narrow point of her nose. Her full lips and the silver gleam of her labret piercing.

"Can you identify the woman in the picture, Mr. Pharaoh?"

An answer drifts from my mouth, but I can't hear my own words. I won't hear them. I refuse.

The man in the suit reaches over and swipes his finger across the surface of the tablet. The picture changes. I only

1

get a glance at the photo before my body violently reacts. My peripheral vision evaporates, and blackness threatens to bleed across my eyes. I can taste the rising bile in my mouth just before I turn and puke.

The suit is speaking, but I can't hear him. He tries to hold my gaze, but the world is receding into blank, lightless nothing. My legs give out. A sharp pain erupts in my shoulder as I hit the linoleum. The floor is cold, or maybe that's just how things are now. Maybe everything is cold.

A horrible, muffled sound cuts through the overwhelming silence —the crying of a desperate animal, or the wailing of a damned soul. My throat, already raw from intermittent crying, throbs with pain, but I barely notice.

The suit is kneeling beside me. It looks like he's yelling, but I can't make out his words. Seconds later a guard appears. He holds my arm down, and the guard jabs me with a syringe.

Whatever's in the needle stings as it courses into my vein. I find myself wondering if it's poison—if he means to euthanize me. I hope so.

The blackness swells. My heart rate slows. The world goes dark.

The sun descends below the Pacific. Pinks, oranges, and purples—celestial hues unique to the California sunset—mock me with their beauty. Or maybe they beckon me to follow the sun beneath the waves into that realm of death where I would already be if I were a braver man.

I snub out a cigarette in the wet sand and let the smoke billow through my nostrils. Cigarettes are such a cowardly and foolish form of suicide. A gun would be much quicker. Just pull the trigger, like ripping off a band-aid. But maybe the cigarettes are part of my penance, along with the booze. Maybe I long to be punished for my failures by the gods of cancer and liver disease.

My phone buzzes in my pocket. Another text message. Dozens of them wait, unanswered.

One from my agent. *I'm so sorry, Nate. I'm here if you need anything.*

Another from Sebastian. *My door's open if you need to jam, or smoke, or if you just don't want to be alone.*

I fling the phone into the ocean. I imagine it skipping a few times, with the up-and-down arc of a sea serpent, before sinking beneath the surface. In reality, it just splashes into the water.

I pull up to the curb in my old 66 Continental and cut the ignition. A sign made up of glass tubes shines in the darkness across the street. Neon red lights spell out the words *Old Ironsides.* Below that, in smaller letters, it says *Mixed* in green and *Drinks* in red.

I don't bother putting the top up as I get out of the car, but I lock the doors out of habit. The neon light reflects off the yellow enamel of my car, creating amber and lemon-lime highlights. I reach into the back seat and grab my guitar case before crossing 10th Street.

A few twenty-somethings lean against the club's brick exterior smoking and shooting the shit about new bands and old records. It's the kind of conversation I used to enjoy. There is a certain level of surrealness listening to their excitement over such simple pleasures. It's like they are completely unaware that the world ended a few days back. I suppose for them it didn't. But it will someday.

One of the kids recognizes me and nods, trying to keep cool. I nod back and a big, goofy smile erupts behind his patchy beard. It feels like ages since I've smiled. He starts whispering to his buddies after I pass by, asking if they know who I am.

I turn the corner and approach the front door of Old Ironsides. A huge mural of an old-timey ship is painted across the front of the building. It's just like I remember when I played here thirty years ago.

The doorman has probably twenty-five years on the kids smoking butts outside, which means he's about my age. It also means he definitely knows who I am, unlike most of the kids lined up out front.

"Oh shit! You're Nathan Pharaoh."

"Yep," I say. "I was hoping I could get good and drunk and play a few songs if you can fit me in."

"Hell yeah, man, of course!" he says with a big grin. "Well, I imagine so, anyway. I can't actually say yes or no, but I'm sure Chucky would love it if you played."

"Cool, man," I say. "I'm gonna grab a drink. Can you just send Chucky over to the bar when you get a second?"

"For sure. Can I get a pic?"

The doorman calls over a waitress and hands his phone to her. I throw my arm over his broad shoulder, but I can't bring myself to fake a smile. He doesn't care. His grin is big enough for the both of us. He pats me on the back, and I head to the bar.

I scan the crowd when I walk in, looking for her as if she's gonna be waiting for me in that lowcut red dress I love. She's

4

not there of course. Not at the bar. Not in the crowd. Not in the world.

I take a seat and lean my guitar case against the bar. A tattoo of a snake slithers up from the bartender's cleavage and coils around her throat. Her blue irises, bisected by a reptilian pupil, regard me coolly.

Her nose, her lips ... they look so much like my wife's. She's almost the spitting image of her, but younger of course, just like ...

No, I'm not ready to think about who she really looks like. Not yet.

As much as she reminds me of Dalia, she lacks all her warmth and charm. There's a glint of cruelty and madness in her serpentine eyes and her expression is cold as ice.

I order a whiskey on the rocks, which she delivers without smile or comment. By my second whiskey, the manager comes over. He introduces himself as Chucky and tells the bartender that my drinks are free. I ask if he can fit me on the night's bill. He's more than happy to accommodate.

People are stealing glances at me and whispering to their friends. Those who didn't recognize me have been clued in by their friends. A tatted-up sound guy comes over and asks if he can set up my Les Paul. I hand him the case and let him know I'll need a stool, a mic, and an amp—just something with a clean channel.

A few people have tried to talk to me, but no one has said anything about my family. I wonder if they know what happened. I wonder if they even know I had a family. Sebastian's the one on the magazines—the guy that the tabloids always tripped over themselves to talk about. He's the one who would bounce from porn star to pop singer, stealing all the headline space he could. I was just the dude in the background playing rhythm, and I liked it that way. I also liked being the guy with just one girl. One perfect girl.

Downing my third shot I realize that the booze isn't making me feel any better. It's not dulling the pain. It's just adding more weight and dragging me down.

The bartender goes to pour me another. I raise my hand to say I've had enough, but she still fills the glass, smiling for the first time. It's a different kind of smirk than everyone else is wearing. Not a star-struck grin or a fake, ass-kissing smile, but a hateful dare. It's like she's challenging me to take the drink—challenging me to step deeper into the dark. I look her in those cold serpentine eyes, and I return her cruel smile with my own *fuck you* grin, then knock back the whiskey and make my way to the stage.

I take my seat on the stage and adjust my guitar. It's been over two decades since I've played in a venue this small. Twenty or so people crowd the stage. Someone yells my name. They all look so excited ... so happy ... so alien. I thought I'd feel something deeper at an intimate performance like this, but I just feel cold. Maybe it's the whiskey or maybe that's just how things are now. Maybe the world's just a colder place.

My left hand forms a diminished D chord. I drag my pick down the strings, letting each note resonate for the slightest bit. There's too much reverb but I kind of dig it. It lends an old Roy Orbison sound to my playing.

I close my eyes and strum another chord, losing touch with everything as the tide of music and whiskey consumes me. The pain gets washed away by my encroaching buzz and the resolving notes. No more shattered family. No more dead wife. No more me. Just the rhythm and the melody.

She kisses down my stomach, her golden hair caressing my bare flesh. I try to tell her how scared I was. I try to tell her how much I love her. The words slur in my mouth. She lifts her head and presses a finger against her lips shushing me. I go quiet and she smiles that crooked smile that melts my heart.

She takes me in her mouth, holding my gaze as she works her head up and down, twisting ever so slightly with each rise and fall. I run my fingers through her hair, and she quickens her pace. Before I can finish, she climbs on top of me and my cock slides into her. She leans over me, teasing me with her lips and tongue. I pull her toward me and kiss her as my hips rise to drive my entire length into her.

"I'm sorry I wasn't there," I say.

She nibbles on my ear.

"You're here now".

We make love all night – that guiltless, clean love that I never knew until her. It's a blur of ecstasy and emotion more powerful than booze or drugs or even rock n' roll.

I open my eyes to a bedroom I've never seen. There's a woman snoring, her head resting on my chest. Her hair is the wrong shade of blonde. My heart physically aches when I realize I wasn't with my wife last night. Bile rises in my throat, and I fight to choke it back down.

I don't remember this chick. Hell, I don't remember leaving Old Ironsides. I can vaguely recall telling someone that I was gonna drive straight across Route 50 until I hit the Atlantic, and them saying I should probably get a good night's sleep first.

It's been a good long while since I got this drunk or hungover. My head is pounding. I do that slow and awkward morning after escape shimmy, trying not to wake whoever is lying on my chest. It shouldn't be a problem if she was as drunk as I was.

It feels like it takes forever, but I finally wiggle away from my one-night stand. The floor is littered with clothes and I have to fish around to find my socks and underwear in the mess. After a minute or two, I give up on my boxers. She can keep them as a trophy.

The walls are lined with horror movie posters and rock n' roll lithographs. While slipping into my jeans, being careful not to zip myself up, I notice a much younger version of myself— like our first major record young—smirking at me from behind baby-face versions of the rest of the band. That arrogant grin on the poster reminds me of what a prick I was before I met my wife and before I had my kid. I flip off my younger self and tiptoe out of the room, carrying my shoes and shirt with me.

It's still dark when I get outside, and I have no clue what time it is. I don't know if I woke up early or if I slept through an entire day. It doesn't really matter, I suppose.

My car is parked at the curb, and my guitar is laid out across the back seat. Thank God for small favors. I start up the engine and flip on the headlights. The beams cut through the darkness, and I follow their light to Route 50.

OCTOBER

The double yellow line guides me through the blackness that encroaches on all sides. My headlights reveal a sign proclaiming a speed limit of 35. Something tells me there aren't any speed traps this far in the desert, but I keep to the needle under 40, if only to conserve gas.

It's been at least an hour since I've seen another car unless you count the wrecked frames of junkers surrendered to the desert sands. I'm not alone out here though. There are things other than people in the cold Nevada night. I see them lurking on the sides of the road, just beyond the peripheral reach of my headlights. Glittering cat eyes and black shapes creeping through blacker darkness.

I turn up the radio, letting Elvis' voice push back the chilling atmosphere of the road. I find myself wondering if The King ever drove down this stretch of highway during his Vegas tenure.

Up ahead there's a great mass of sand, maybe twenty feet high. The dump truck beside it tells me it's not a dune, but something man-made—a staging area or a drop point for a quarry probably. I must be getting close to Austin. Austin, Nevada that is, not Texas.

The road curves and an interstate sign reminds me that I'm still heading across US-50, the loneliest road in America. I haven't been this deep in Nevada in longer than I care to think about. Not since we got our first big paycheck. I told my old man that I'd buy him a house anywhere in the world. To this day I can't tell you why he chose to retire in a ghost town in the middle of the Mojave. If I had to wager a guess, I'd say that after mom passed he couldn't stand looking at the ocean or anything else that stood to remind him of her.

I used to think it was cowardly, how he just turned his back on the world to hide in the wastes of the Southwest. Now I get it. Sometimes the hurt is just too much and you do whatever you can to dial it down.

LED lights mounted high on metal posts illuminate a Chevron station coming up on the right. I pass by a derelict building that looks like a saloon from a spaghetti western sound stage, as I pull into the gas station.

A ragged strip of duct tape is covering the credit card slot. The lights are on in the station, and the sign reads *open*. When I step out of my Lincoln, the cold of the desert night hits me and goosebumps erupt across my arms. My breath takes the form of smoke in the air, and I snatch my leather jacket from the back seat.

A bell rings as I enter the gas station. Not an electric chime, but a leather strap with sleighbells. A grizzled biker-looking guy behind the register looks up from a tattered paperback copy of *The Odyssey*. His leathery skin is a dark, earthy tone of red. A black cowboy hat sits atop his wild mane of ebony hair.

The inside of the Chevron is more modern than one might expect from an unincorporated ghost town on the loneliest road in America. It looks like a regular old mini-mart, same as you might come across in any city across the country.

"What can I do for you?" he asks.

"I just want to fill up on pump one, and maybe grab a six-pack."

The biker points down an aisle of chips and candy bars toward a wall of coolers at the back of the store. It's slim pickings regarding beer. Bud and Michelob for the most part. I used to love Budweiser, but I became a beer snob somewhere along the way, and now I can't stomach the shit. I guess wealth has made a prick of me in that way.

I settle for a six-pack of Yuengling, the best option in the cooler, and rest it on the register next to a plastic Jack O' Lantern filled with lollipops and Smarties. While the biker behind the counter scans my purchase and does whatever secret things he needs to unlock the pump, I find myself staring at the animal skull adorning his hat. It almost looks like that of a tiny dog, but not quite. The snout is extended too far, and the shape isn't quite right.

It's not just the skull that looks off. Up this close, I notice some odd things about the biker himself. The tops of his ears are squared off, almost like someone had taken a razor and sliced off the crown of each. And his eyes—they shift between grey and black and sandy brown. His gaze reminds me of a storm.

"Go fill up," he says. "You can pay when you're done."

He speaks quietly, but there is a low, thunderous quality to his voice. I nod and head out to fill my tank, leaving the six-pack on the counter.

When I go back outside my eyes are no longer accustomed to the darkness, and everything beyond the glow of the Chevron station's lights is a black abyss. As I pump gas into the hungry Lincoln my mind begins populating the darkness with monsters. Vampires with teeth like obsidian arrowheads.

Methhead bikers wielding chains and shotguns. Dead wives and daughters urging me to follow them into the darkness.

The nozzle clicks to a stop. The Lincoln's thirst is sated. I screw the gas cap on and return the nozzle to its home on the pump. The monsters call from the black night, but I turn my back on them and go to settle up with the biker working the counter.

The bell rings again as I enter. The clerk calls out what I owe him without looking up from his book. I walk over to the counter and drop a hundred-dollar bill. "Keep the change," I tell him.

"They're real you know," he says.

"Who are?"

"Those things in the darkness. Whatever you brought here with you …well … you brought them here with you."

I've never been good at hiding my feelings and I feel a flush of anger overtake my face. Does he think he's funny? Or deep? Some third-shift, gas station philosopher?

I grab my six-pack and turn to leave. Fuck this guy and his *spook-the-tourist* bullshit.

"Stick to the road, Nathan Pharaoh," he calls after me. "You don't want to meet the things waiting in the wastes."

The road curves ahead, like a slithering beast through the nearly deserted town of Austin, Nevada. My headlights reveal boarded-up houses, failed businesses, and empty lots. They all vanish into nothing as soon as I pass by. A few dots of electric light show here and there in the distance. The main drag is dark and seems mostly deserted.

A church materializes on my right, its wooden steeple stretching high enough into the sky that any cross that might adorn the top is lost to the night. There aren't a lot of landmarks here and I vaguely remember the church from the last time I visited. I think this is where I turn right to get to Dad's house.

I glide off of Route 50 and onto some side street where the burning grins of Jack o' Lanterns greet me from the few occupied homes. Despite the Halloween decorations, I don't see any trick-or-treaters. Maybe it's too late. Maybe there just aren't any children in this town. I can't imagine choosing to raise a family in a place like this. I keep it under 25 anyway, just in case some masked kid rushes out into the street.

I take a slow left at the end of the road. Someone pulls aside a curtain from a window at the house on the corner. An ancient face peeks through the glass and watches me drive by. I can't tell if they are curious or distrustful. Probably both.

A few blocks down the next street and I pull into a big lot of sand and brush. Dad's place sits twenty feet back, a big wooden house set on a foundation of yellow brick. I'm not sure what you'd call architecture. Modernist maybe? The front of his place is rounded off and it looks like one of those 1960s Hollywood Hills-type houses, but the hillbilly bootleg version. The facade is made of wooden slats instead of the painted concrete you'd see in LA, and there are normal-sized casement windows in place of giant walls of glass. Still, you can tell what the architect was going for. As I walk up the driveway, beers in hand, it occurs to me that this house was probably Dad's way of feeling like a rock star in his own right.

The lights are off and the door is locked. Dad's not here. I fumble through the keys on my ring, looking for the spare that he gave me so many years ago. A twinge of guilt washes over me as I slide the key into the lock and think of how few times I've had cause to use it.

It's dark inside the house, but I can make out a few familiar shapes in the murk. A framed LP of my first album is mounted over the fireplace. A coat rack stands to my right, Dad's signature Derby hat hanging from one arm. Dominating the room is a 1970's style sectional. It's set up around a coffee table made from a slice of a redwood trunk.

"Hey, old man," I call into the darkened house. "The prodigal son returns."

I take a seat on the sectional and kick off my boots. The sofa feels nice after sitting in a car for so long. I place the six-pack on the table and fish a ziplock bag of mushrooms from my pocket. The taste of the mushrooms causes me to grimace, so I pop open a Yuengling to wash them down.

It's a futile effort, but I scrape my tongue against my teeth trying to get the taste out of my mouth. Giving up, I close my eyes and lean back, allowing the cushions to comfort my body and the mushrooms to comfort my soul.

The drive here was long and I'm more tired than I realized. I drift into a half-sleep and a horror film plays out on the backs of my eyelids. My wife glares at me with empty eyes, coiled serpents dragging her beneath cold waters. Black poison tears run down her cheeks, blistering her skin.

"Why weren't you there, Nathan?" she asks, her blue lips unmoving. "It didn't have to be this way."

I shake the image from my head, but it dissolves into something even worse … another face, so much like hers, but this time with the eyes of a snake. It doesn't ask me why I wasn't there. It hisses the words as an accusation.

"You weren't there!"

My eyes shoot open and a cry escapes my lips. My father is sitting beside me, a look of concern on his weathered face. He places a hand on my knee and asks if I'm okay.

"No, Dad. I'm not." I take a swallow of my beer and fight back the tears that are welling in my eyes. "I'm really not."

"I know, Nate. I'm so sorry, my little king."

"I wish you could have met them … I wish I'd have taken the time …"

He puts his arm around my shoulder and the dam breaks. I sob like a child as he hugs me tight. I never thought my old man would hold me like this again, but I never expected I'd need him to.

"I should have been there, but that's the story of my life, right? I'm a selfish prick and I should have been there for Dalia when it happened. I should have been there for you when Mom passed. I should have been there when …"

"That's enough, Nate. Ain't no changing the past."

"But I fucked up so bad, Dad. I should have seen it coming. I wasn't even in the same country when it happened. I never said goodbye. I never said sorry."

Nausea overtakes me and I choke back a throat full of puke. Maybe it's the grief. Maybe it's the mushrooms or the beer. Maybe it's all three.

"Do you know what I'd do for the chance to say goodbye? For one more kiss? One more dance?"

"Would one more be enough?" he asks. I don't say anything because we both know the answer.

Dad slaps me on the back, then grabs a beer and stands up. He motions for me to follow, and grabs his hat from the coat rack.

"It's Halloween, boy. Let's go dance with the dead."

The road to the cemetery outside of town had been lost to the desert sands. The tires of my Continental kick a dusty aura up around us as we drive. I can barely see where I'm going, and I have no notion of where the road heads, but my father assures me I'm going the right way.

"Just up ahead here, on the right."

It takes me a few seconds to see what he's talking about, but there it is—a crumbling graveyard surrounded by a rusted iron gate. I turn the car so that the headlights shine right into the cemetery. Eroded grave markers poke out from the baked earth like crooked teeth in a diseased mouth.

"I recognize this place. It's where you asked to be buried."

"They don't put folks in here no more, but I figured my rock star son could pull some strings."

"Why this place? Why the middle of the desert?"

"It makes me feel close to your mother."

"But Mom's buried in Corvallis?"

"Yeah, but your mom and I met in Nevada. We fell in love in the desert. As bad as things got between us over the years, as miserable as we both were when she was sick, I knew there was always something better of us left here … something I wanted to be able to go back to."

I go to kill the engine, but Dad stops me.

"Leave it running, and put on some music … something you can dance to."

I start the Elvis disc over and crank the volume. Strings swell and pianos follow.

Dad steps out of the car and walks toward the graveyard. He merges with the windblown sand in my headlights, then reforms as he steps out of their path.

"Be mindful of what you bring in here with you, Nate. You reap what you sow, and all that."

I follow my father into the cemetery and I watch my mother materialize in the moonlight as Elvis's voice bellows from the speakers of my car. She looks as she did when I was young—the kind and beautiful woman who raised me, not the bitter revenant that cancer turned her into during that final year. My father takes her hand and they both grin like teenagers in love.

It breaks my heart to look at her—the mixture of grief and guilt. I wasn't there for her, just like I wasn't there for my own family. I was too busy filling stadiums to visit her when she was sick, but at least I made it to the funeral, right? I'm a hell of a son.

I want to hug her. I want to tell her I'm sorry for being such a self-centered piece of shit. But this she's not here for me. She's here for Dad.

There's a tap on my shoulder, gentle, but cold. I turn and all thoughts of my parents melt away as I look upon Dalia's face. She smiles, her eyes glittering with moonlight and love.

"You gonna ask me to dance?"

I take Dalia's hand in mine. Her skin is colder than the desert night and softer than satin. I pull her tight, even as her touch drains the warmth from my body.

"If I made you feel second best," I sing the words along with the King. "Girl, I'm sorry, I was blind."

Dalia rests her head against my chest as we sway beneath the desert moon. My breath comes out in hot bursts of white mist and I can feel my heart trying to break free from my chest—trying to go home—trying to go to her.

The song ends and another begins. An arpeggio gives way to a deep voice singing of wise men and fools. I sing along, meaning every word.

People say that love at first sight is bullshit. Maybe it is just a chemical reaction—a trick of the brain to get us to fuck and breed. All I know is that time stopped when I first saw her fierce, blue eyes framed by locks of silken gold. Nothing was ever the same after that moment. The whole world was monochrome in comparison.

I want to tell her all of that, but my words never come out the way I think them. That's why I play music. I stick to my strengths and keep singing to her. Everything I want to say is in the song.

"I can't help falling in love with you."

We spin between headstones and into the beams of the Continental's headlights. Dalia vanishes into dust and sand. I panic and grasp at the empty space before me. I cry her name, stumble over a grave and fall to the ground, away from the light.

Dalia is there on top of me as if she were never gone. She laughs and places a kiss on my cheek. Her lips burn like dry ice on my skin, but I don't flinch. The pain of her dead kiss is so much kinder than the agony of her absence.

She stands and helps me to my feet. We hold each other and sway as I watch my parents do the same at the far end of the cemetery. Dad winks at me and I wink back, the same way we would when sharing a wonderful secret when I was a kid.

The singing fades and the piano notes resolve. The opening to *You Gave Me a Mountain* plays and I spin Dalia. When I pull her back she's different. Her face is younger, nearly childlike and her blue eyes have been swapped with those of a snake.

I realize that my wife is gone. This girl I now hold has my wife's face, but her reptilian eyes hold nothing but chaos and hate. Tattooed serpents coil over her shoulders and down her arms, totemic of her soul.

The music warps. The notes swing out of key and the vocal harmony falls out of time.

"Deprived of the love of a father," she sings along with the song, hissing the words with no sense of meter or harmony. "Blamed for the loss of his wife."

I close my eyes to her. She looks so much like Dalia—the same mouth and same nose—but otherwise warped and wrong. Looking upon her reminds me of my every shortcoming and all my failures.

I struggle to break away from the snake-woman's grip, but she holds me tight, forcing us into a chaotic waltz among the gravestones. The vipers inked into her arms come to life. They tear free from her flesh and lash out toward me.

Dripping fangs pierce through my jacket and into my flesh, pumping out burning venom. The toxin permeates my skin, my muscle, and my blood. Deeper still, it penetrates my soul.

My foot catches on a gravestone. We tumble back, our bodies entwined. White starbursts explode before me as my skull slams into an overturned piece of slate.

The serpentine woman holds me to the ground and her vipers continue to snap at me. I try to call for my parents to help, but the venom steals my breath. They dance in the dark, lost in one another and oblivious to my struggle.

I kick against the ground dragging myself along, trying to escape the graveyard. The girl with Dalia's face holds on to me. Her grip is inescapable. It's past regret. It's terminal illness. It's the tragedy that waits for us all.

My screams and grunts fall flat in the desert night. They don't carry or echo but die just beyond my lips.

The cemetery gate is close. I can see the rotted cast iron bars where the headlights of my car cut through the darkness. I drag myself toward the graveyard's edge, pulling the terrible woman and her snakes along with me. The headlights wash over us as I get near the gate and the vipers dissolve into sand and smoke. My attacker lets go with a hiss and retreats into the night, away from the cones of light emanating from my car.

There's something warm running down my neck. I reach for the back of my head, to the spot that aches from my fall. My hair is sticky and wet. I look at my hand to find it covered in red.

Vertigo kicks in and the world begins a clumsy pirouette. A cyclone of monstrous shadows fills the darkness beyond my headlights---slithering phantasms, desert vampires, and demons born of Mojave tragedy.

The words of the biker at the filling station echo in my mind.

Stick to the road, Nathan Pharaoh. You don't want to meet the things waiting in the wastes.

I scoot my way back until I'm leaning against the rusted gate. My eyes are heavy ... too heavy to keep open. I thank whatever gods might exist that I didn't shut off the car, and I pray the Lincoln's headlights are enough to protect me until dawn. The song on my stereo changes and my prayer descends into a mumbled sing-along with *Heartbreak Hotel* as I fade into the oblivion of sleep.

☥

I wake up in the graveyard, the sun halfway between the eastern horizon and its noontime peak. There are no monsters or ghosts in the sun-bleached landscape. There's no music and no dancing dead. It's silent, save for the sound of the Mojave winds and my own aching groans.

My mouth is dry and my skin is slick with sweat. I stumble to my feet, still dizzy from the night before. My car is parked outside the gate, the engine still running, the beams of its headlights lost beneath the glare of the morning sun.

I cut through the collapsed part of the fence and grab a hot can of beer from the back seat. It opens with a hiss that reminds me of the girl with the serpentine eyes. The bitter taste is like a mouthful of warm venom. Nonetheless, I suck down a greedy swallow.

Beer in hand, I cross back into the cemetery. There is one grave that stands out from the rest— a marble headstone amid a forest of slate. The others are broken and worn at the edges, some overturned. Their inscriptions are almost unreadable. While the wind and the sand have worn away some of the marble's shine, this stone is pristine in comparison to the rest.

I kneel before the marble headstone and dust the sand away from the face of the grave. My fingers graze across the inscription and the letters feel rough in comparison to the polished surface.

Here Lies Seth Farrow, beloved husband and father.

I take another sip of the hot lager, then pour the rest over Dad's grave.

November

The gray twilight hangs over the flat expanse that stretches out on either side of the road. Scraggly brush clings to life in the inhospitable soil, barely managing to keep itself on the right side of existence. Powerlines stretch across miles of wooden crosses. No gasping, crimson-browed demi-gods look down from them. No surrogate sufferers offer salvation.

The Romans used to crucify thieves and highwaymen on the side of roads as reminders of transgression and punishment. I muse that the crossed pillars following Route 50 serve a similar purpose. They're emblems of that which we've lost and omens of tragedy yet to come. The crosses are here to remind anyone traveling down the loneliest road, just how alone they are.

Or maybe they're just powerlines. Maybe I've been alone with my thoughts for too long.

The dusky horizon looks more like a movie backdrop than real-life—distant mountains obscured by titanic clouds far down this never-ending road. It makes me wonder if this journey has a point, if it has an end, or if this is my life now—an endless road trip, the kind I'd dreamed of when I first imagined playing in bands. I couldn't wait to leave home and hit the highway when I was young. Now I'm old, and all I want is to go home, but there is no home anymore. The gods of irony are looking down on me with cruel smiles, I'm sure.

I pass through Hinkley, a sparsely settled village where run-down houses and rusting farm equipment poke out from the earth like stray tufts of fur on a mange-ridden dog. It's not a ghost town in the same way that Austin, Nevada is, but it's not quite alive either.

A dying pickup truck with Utah plates drives by in the other lane. The driver bears no expression and no music echoes from the cab. The only sound from the truck is the grumble of its ancient exhaust. I look in my side mirror after it passes. Three laborers sit in the bed of the truck, huddled together in threadbare jackets. They're smoking cigarettes—courting cancer like it's a rich lover come to rescue them from their daily toil.

The skyline turns from gray to navy over the next few miles, then from navy to black. Night cloaks the world with an unsettling quickness. Stray beams of silver moonlight cut through the black clouds stretched across the sky and the world beyond the periphery of my headlights vanishes. I see only the crimson glow of my taillights in the rearview. All else is emptiness. The road feels like a crumbling bridge, threatening to collapse beneath me if I can't outrun it.

A voice hisses beneath the static-laced gospel music playing on the radio. It whispers my failures and sins. It urges me to veer off into the darkness. It tells me to lean on the gas and careen toward an oncoming pole.

I follow the twisting center line of the road out to the edge of Hinkley. The cold, neon light of a *Blue Moon* sign beckons from the window of a tiny bar. The air around the bar wavers like a heat mirage despite the first bite of winter in the air.

I pull into the dirt parking lot. I tell myself it's because I have to piss, but that's bullshit and I know it.

I want to drink.

I want to drink until I forget my name.

I want to drink until my liver fails and my heart stops.

The lot is fuller than one would expect for a bar in the middle of nowhere. A few bikes are lined up outside the front window while dust-covered cars sit haphazardly parked. A '55 Corvette with chipped yellow paint sits beside an olive-drab Jeep. Dings and rot holes mar the gorgeous curves of an original F-series pickup. The flat tires of a Plymouth Business Coup merge into the packed earth. The place is like the car show of the living dead.

Each vehicle displays an out-of-state plate, everywhere from Oregon to Rhode Island. The bar isn't for the few sad souls that reside in Hinkley. No, it's a den for travelers—a place to drown whatever sorrows caused us to set out on our cursed odysseys.

It's dim inside the roadside tavern. The only light comes from a few overhead bulbs and the neon signs hanging in the windows and over the shelves of booze. Three simian-faced bikers play a game of cutthroat in the corner and pass a bottle of Jack Daniels around the pool table. Dead-eyed men stare into shot glasses and amber pints.

A dark-skinned bartender nods to me as I approach the bar. His long silver mohawk is brushed to one side, forming a crescent veil over half his face. He stares at me with cataract white eyes. I can't figure out if they are giving off their own glow or just reflecting ambient light.

"What will it be, Pharaoh?"

He knows my name, but I suppose lots of people do.

"Beer. Whatever's strongest."

He pops the cap off a bottle and places it in front of me. The label reads *Heket*. The name is printed in a papyrus font above a cartoon goddess with the face of a frog.

"Sorry for your loss."

I nod and take a swallow of the beer. It's cold and soothing. There's a real flavor to it, a pleasant contrast to the watered-down gas station piss I've been drinking lately.

A familiar song comes on the jukebox. It's one of mine—a bullshit ballad about heartache before I ever knew what it meant. I smirk and cringe, anticipating the pretentious lyrics.

A haggard man in a wrinkled suit is leaning over the jukebox. A single tear runs down his cheek as he mouths my lyrics. I guzzle the rest of my beer and walk over to him.

"This song ain't worth crying over," I tell him. "It's a sham. Commercially manufactured grief."

The man sneers at me, his bared teeth framed by salt and pepper stubble. The sorrow burning behind his bloodshot, jaundiced eyes is as familiar to me as the music playing over the speakers.

"How would you know?"

"I wrote it."

The man chuckles and the dam breaks. He stumbles to the bar, rivers of tears running down his face. Stray sobs interrupt his hysterical laughter.

I sit down beside him. The bartender places a beer in front of each of us.

"You don't look like the guy in the music video," he says after gathering his composure.

"Sebastian hogged the camera. I was the guy playing guitar in the background. Name's Nathan Pharaoh."

"Kevin King."

We clink our bottles and drink. I reflect on my words as sung by Sebastian. The song seems like blasphemy now—a belittlement of genuine tragedy. The gravity of soul-shaking

26

heartbreak is too powerful to capture in poetic phrasing. It can't be expressed through minor-key arpeggios or the wailing string bends of a slow guitar solo.

Kevin King and I don't need a conversation to know the nature of each other's grief. It's written across both our faces. Remnants of shattered souls. Shards of broken families.

King pulls a snubnose revolver out from beneath his blazer. The sight of it startles and excites me. There's a dangerous beauty to it, not just in its sleek dimensions and shining chrome, but in the promise of oblivion it represents.

"It belonged to Elvis, believe it or not," King tells me.

"Bullshit."

"Cross my heart," he says, drawing an X across his chest with one finger. "I bought it at an auction for fifty grand, back when blowing money on stupid shit still felt good."

King hands me the pistol. It's heavier than it looks. The weight is comforting, as is the cool touch of the steel.

"I've always loved guns," King tells me. "I used to have these terrible fantasies of sickos breaking into my home … trying to hurt my family. I wanted it to happen. I wanted to be a Hollywood hero and go all Charlie Bronson on some Charlie Manson creep."

King chugs the rest of his beer and signals for another. He holds his hand out. I give the gun back to him.

"When tragedy came … when this cruel, devouring world came for my family … well, the gun didn't help one bit." He retrieves a single bullet from his breast pocket and loads it into the gun. "I still love guns, but I don't see them as weapons anymore. They're more like keys … or maybe plane tickets. I don't know, I'm shit with metaphors."

King spins the cylinder and slams it back into place with

a flick of his wrist. He pulls back the hammer and places the muzzle against his temple.

"The point is, it's my only way home, now."

The hammer clicks and I let out a curse, but no explosion follows. My heart is in my throat. My hands are trembling.

"Better luck next time," one of the bikers shouts from over at the pool table. The others start howling and slamming their cues against the table. They break into a chorus of laughter.

I stare at the gun, thinking of it like King suggested … as a key. Could a few grams of lead be the answer to all my problems?

"Why spin the chamber? Why not just do the deed?"

"Why didn't you drive your car into a telephone pole on your way here?"

I don't have a good answer. Maybe there's too much agency in suicide without an element of chance. Maybe I'm too much of a coward.

King places the gun on the bar. I pick it up and give the cylinder a twirl. The bartender shakes his head at me, but I ignore him and slam the cylinder into place. I turn the gun on myself and pull the trigger. I'm met with a harmless click. Adrenaline surges through me. It makes the world spin and sends tremors through my body.

The bartender places two more bottles in front of us as King asks me if I have any children. I don't know how to answer the question, so I don't. Instead, I place the pistol in front of him.

"I always said my son was my life, but I was full of shit. That was my excuse for working so much—so I could provide for him—so I could give him the things I never had. The thing is, I spent so much time in offices and board rooms, that I missed his whole childhood. I can remember every software acronym and corporate procedure from my job, but sometimes I struggle remembering what his laugh sounded like."

King spins the chamber and presses the pistol against his skull again. He smiles, but it's filled with sadness.

"I just want to hear my little boy laugh again."

He pulls the trigger. No whammy. The bikers jeer in the background. He curses under his breath and hands me the gun.

I start thinking about what things I might have forgotten about Dalia. I can still hear her voice and the unique intonations of her different moods. My mind can still conjure images of her smile ... the way her front teeth protruded lower than the rest ... the way her smile curled up higher on the left side of her mouth. But what about the sound of her snoring? Is it as I remember, or am I substituting stock sound clips?

And about Cleo? Shit, I haven't even allowed myself to breathe her name since everything happened. My wife's death was painful enough. But Cleo ... God, it's so much worse ... so nightmarishly fucking complex. It's like I lost her twice.

I try to think of my little girl's face, as it was when she was young, but it's gone. Her eyes are vertical slits of obsidian. Her teeth are fangs dripping with venom.

I can't do this. I can't think about her. I take my turn with the pistol, praying that I find the slug.

Click.

The bar echoes with taunts as the bikers grow impatient for blood. I lower my head and let my hair hang over my face. It covers my tears and my shame. I slide the gun over to King.

"Maybe we can't die, because we're already in hell." King holds up the gun and admires the blue gleam of neon light on its barrel. "Maybe it doesn't matter how many times we play this game. The bullet will never find us because we're already dead."

He pulls the trigger before I have time to ponder his suggestion and his head explodes into a fine, red mist. The bartender shakes his head and wipes the blood from the bar. A cacophony of howls erupts from the group of bikers as they leap onto the pool table. One slams a striped ball into a solid, while another humps his cue.

King's corpse lays slumped on the floor. The gun didn't open any doors. It wasn't a key or a plane ticket. It didn't take him home to his family.

The scrambled hunks of brain on the wall—that's all that was left of his wife and his little boy. They'd lived on only in his memories of the tender moments and tiny tragedies. Now the last remnants of them are extinct. In his pain, King assigned them to oblivion.

The bikers swarm around Kevin King's dead body. They snap at each other and fight over handfuls of gray matter. Blood and brain dribble down their chins as they gobble up bits of his ruined mind.

I thank whatever gods may be that King won our game of roulette. I grab the gun from the floor and flee into the cold night.

A yellowed tabloid blows across the dirt lot. For a moment I think it's Dalia's picture on the front page, but the woman is too gaunt and frail. I realize it's Cleo. Even beneath the over-size sunglasses, I can tell that she looks old beyond her years.

I lean down and grab the paper. The headline fills me with guilt, anger, and disgust.

The Tragic Last Days of a Rock N' Roll Heiress.

My daughter walks beside a robed figure in the image. A

charlatan smile sits above his square jaw. They both wear the same necklace—a metallic serpent curled up in the center of a pyramid.

I look at King's gun—*The King's* gun—then back at the picture of the man with my daughter. Bile rises in my throat. The pity party's over. Now it's time to take care of business.

"TCB, baby."

DECEMBER

Sunlight pierces through an ice-encrusted window on the western side of the room. It wakes me up and I fumble for my sunglasses which rest somewhere between the empty wine glasses and crushed beer cans on the table beside me. Pain radiates down my spine as I sit up. I curse the shitty loveseat that I've been sleeping on for the better part of a week.

The room is littered with the snoring, half-naked bodies of the self-hating bourgeoisie. Trust fund punk rockers, art school dropouts, and strippers with enough ink to put a down payment on a house are sprawled out on the floor and curled up in lush chairs. We've all been here for days, trapped by the blizzard that's been tearing across the mountains. I get the feeling that most of them would have hung around anyway, at least until the free booze stopped flowing and the cocaine ran out.

I step around the sleeping bodies, making my way to the window. It's hard to see outside, through the ice and snow coating the glass, so I crack it open and let the December cold wash over me as I light up a cigarette.

Icicles hang from power lines and the landscape is blanketed in a pristine coat of white, accented only by black strips of asphalt. The storm has finally passed, and the roads are clear. It's time to go.

Couch Surfing Through the 12 Chambers of Hell

I start salivating and it takes me a moment to consciously notice the sweet smell of maple sausages and the strong scent of fresh-brewed coffee. I make my way back to the couch, passing a sleeping, topless woman curled up on top of a baby grand. I sit down to lace up my boots, then head into the kitchen.

"Morning, Nate."

Leo Schesmu, an old friend, stands at the gas range, shaking a skillet over the flame. Leo is an old man ... older than me at least, by ten years or more. We crashed here with him on our second tour, once on our way out east, and again on the way home. He had to be in his thirties back then, which puts him in his sixties now, not that you can tell by looking at him.

Despite his age and the non-stop bacchanalia he's been living for as long as I've known him, his face isn't marred by lines of age and his thick shock of golden hair hasn't thinned a bit. He carries himself with almost royal bearing and possesses the type of dense muscle you only see on guys who've served a long stint in prison.

Most people who approach life like an endless party grow old quickly. Smoke yellows their teeth and liver failure yellows their eyes. Their skin and hair go to shit. They waste away on dope or get fat from beer. Not Leo. He's Peter Pan, always keeping up with the ever-changing roster of younger partygoers that come and go from his mountaintop Neverland palace.

"What time is it?" I ask.

"Who knows?" Leo shrugs. "I don't worry about that sort of thing."

His accent is strange. I could never place it. Not quite British. Not quite Australian. South African maybe? What the hell kind of surname is Schesmu?

"Can I get some of that caffeine?"

Leo rests the pan on the range and pours me a cup of black coffee. He offers to add in a splash of whiskey, but I decline. I take the mug and sit down at the kitchen table, watching the steam swirl in the air.

"I take it you're gonna be on your way now that the snow has stopped."

"Yeah, I think it's time for me to get going, Leo."

He nods as he tips the sausages out of the pan, onto a plate, and places them in front of me. I thank him and take a bite. They taste better than they should and I realize that I've been living exclusively off of beer and cigarettes for the past few days.

"Don't feel like I'm rushing you out. You're welcome to stay as long as you like."

"I appreciate the hospitality."

"If you want my opinion, a few more days of hedonism would do you a world of good," Leo says picking a bottle of red wine from a rack near the fridge and pouring himself a glass. "There is something quite restorative about wine."

Leo motions toward a sleeping stripper in the other room. "Something quite restorative about love, as well." Her firm, silicone tits rise and fall with each breath. She's young enough to be my daughter.

"That's not love, Leo."

"Neither is revenge." He frowns as he speaks, then tosses more sausages onto a cutting board.

"What are you talking about?

Leo grabs a massive cleaver and cuts the sausages down the center. The blade bites into the wooden cutting board with each strike. There's a sizzle as he nudges the food off the cutting board and into the pan.

"You didn't drive out to Colorado to party with an old

friend. You're here because of Cleo. You're going after that snake-cult nutter she shacked up with."

There's no need to say anything. We both know the truth. I take a sip of my coffee and a drag of my cigarette.

"Running up on that compound like Clint Eastwood ain't gonna bring Cleo or Dalia back, my man. Plus, you're a rock star, not an action hero. These people you plan on tussling with— they aren't stoner hippies living in a mountain commune. These are sick, dangerous motherfuckers. We're talking meth-head tweakers with a religious hard-on for chaos and death."

The steam from my coffee takes the shape of a serpent. I think of my daughter—what she did to my wife—what she did to herself.

"There has to be some kind of justice."

Leo places his hand on my shoulder and brings his face close to mine. He locks eyes with me, a sad smile on his face.

"No man, there doesn't have to." His breath stinks of wine. "Sometimes bad shit happens and there's no fixing it. You can't kill pain with a bullet or blade. You can only drown it or wait for it to fade."

The white sky is pregnant with another storm and the horizon nearly blends in with the snowcapped mountains. All is silent, save for the growl of my engine.

The dashboard clock tells me that it's nearly three in the afternoon. Today is the winter solstice, so I should get to the church compound just before sunset.

The road is clear. Plows have come and gone and salt coats the asphalt. Still, I keep the needle under 30. Route 50 winds back and forth here, and the flimsy guardrail isn't likely to stop my Continental from going off the cliff if I lose control.

A month ago I would have welcomed that fate—a fiery death at the bottom of a scenic ravine. Maybe I still will when this is all over

An hour out from Leo's place, I see a road sign for Monarch Pass. I'm close. Another mile goes by and I turn off the highway, up a private access road. A plow has been through here, but the unsalted ground is still white and treacherous. My tires struggle to find purchase on the packed snow.

Signs screwed into tree trunks declare *No Trespassing* and *Private Property*. Twisting, looping sigils are carved into the bark of pine trees on either side of the road. The designs are scabbed over with resin and remind me of scarified flesh.

A steel barricade blocks the path up ahead. I put the car in park and step out to investigate. A chain and padlock keep the rusted bar from swinging open. It looks like I'm walking from here on out.

I go back to the car to grab my leather jacket and retrieve the gun I got from King—Elvis' gun—from my glove box. I make sure it's loaded and find myself wishing I'd had the forethought to purchase more ammo. I'll just have to make every shot count.

Pistol in hand, I duck under the barricade. The snow crunches beneath my boots, and I mumble four-letter words. Even as the sun fades below the western horizon and darkness falls over the landscape, I fear that my black clothes stand in too deep a contrast against the ice and snow.

The uphill road levels off and I get my first view of the compound. Trailers and prefab shacks form zig-zag avenues across the property, turning it into a chaotic maze. Voices sing in disharmony from somewhere I can't see. The song echoes off the buildings, each voice in a different key and meter.

An orange haze hangs over the compound, emanating from somewhere near the center. Trails of smoke rise over the buildings and fade into the gray, winter night.

I creep through the twisting rows of trailers, careful not to slip on black ice or packed snow. Elvis' gun trembles in my hand and I slow before each open doorway, weary of what danger may lurk on the other side. To my relief, the buildings all seem to be empty.

The cacophonous song is my beacon. I follow it through the labyrinthine compound, turning left past the rusted corpse of a school bus, then right beneath a trellised archway bridging two trailers. The sound grows louder and increasingly terrible with each step I take toward its singers.

Shadows dance on the snow ahead of me—twisting, black tendrils with burning, orange penumbras. I crouch low and keep tight to the wall of a dilapidated shack. The volume of the singing is almost intolerable now.

I peek around the corner and there I see them—a gaggle of lunatics, dancing naked in the freezing night, their writhing bodies illuminated by the shifting light of a massive bonfire. Their lithe forms slither upright and the snakes tattooed on the flesh of each person seem to move of their own accord.

A round boulder sits in the middle of the dancing crowd. It is painted like an old, sepia-toned globe but wrapped in the coils of a serpent, like something out of a World War 2 propaganda poster. Standing on the boulder is the fiend from the newspaper clippings—the devil who seduced my daughter and poisoned her soul.

His naked body is thin and lean, his movements fluid and hypnotic. He sings and postures atop the boulder as if he's a rock star performing for a stadium full of fans. It makes me ill to watch.

The fever of religious ecstasy distracts the sinister congregation from my presence. I raise the King's pistol and place the sights on the leader's chest. Visions of Cleo and Dalia flash through my head, first how they were when our family was whole, then how they looked after tragedy struck.

Tears fill my eyes. With trembling hands, I pull the trigger. The singing falters at the pistol's report. All eyes look up toward their leader, then toward me. It takes a moment for it to set in that I missed. By that point, the lunatics are rushing at me.

I turn and run. The rows of trailers branch off in different directions. I rush down the nearest lane as the naked cultists scream for my blood. My boots skid on a patch of ice and I crash into the mesh walls of a chicken coop sandwiched between aluminum sheds.

Risking a glance backward, I see the insane mob gaining on me. I scramble to my feet and run as fast as I can. The chickens I disturbed squawk and beat their wings, adding to the cacophonous screams of my pursuers.

The avenue twists around a rocky outcropping and comes to a dead-end—a cul de sac of makeshift structures anchored into a small cliff face. I curse myself for taking a wrong turn and scramble up one of the slanted, sheet metal roofs.

The cultists pursue me with reckless abandon. In their bloodlust, some slip and fall on the slick, winter ground. Others trample their clumsy brethren, either unaware or unconcerned with them.

I scoot up on the roof until my back is against the cliff. I fire the pistol and hit one of them in the shoulder. I don't get to shoot again. One clambers up the roof and grasps my foot. He drags me down. I lose my breath as I slam down on the packed snow. The gun falls from my grip and skitters across the ice, well out of my reach.

A fist strikes my cheek. A foot connects with my ribs. My nerves explode with pain as a flurry of blows falls upon me. I try to stand, but my breath still won't come. I curl into a ball as they kick, claw, and bite. With each strike, the cold and the night seep deeper into me until the world goes dark.

I wake up to Dalia's face. She's topless, save for a necklace of intricate gold and pearl beadwork that nearly covers her chest. She stands above me, but her eyes are set on my body, rather than my face. Her hands are busy. I can't tell what she's doing.

"Dalia …" My voice is barely a whisper.

She turns her gaze toward mine and the corner of her lip curls upward.

"Shush. Go back to sleep, Nathan."

Sharp pain goes through my arm as she tugs at something. I moan and grimace. She apologizes.

"What are you doing?" I ask.

"Putting you back together."

I raise my head and look over my prone body. I find that I've been dismembered—chopped up into bits and laid across a stone altar. Dalia's hands work deftly, sewing my bicep to my shoulder.

"What happened?"

"You picked a fight you couldn't win." She leans in and rips

the thread with her teeth before tying it off. "Not sure what you were thinking. Your strength has never been in your fists, Love."

"You were my strength."

"Your strength is the passion that burns in your every cell and shines in every note you play." Dalia places her hand on a piece of my chest. "Your strength is your heart."

"You are my heart."

I try to reach up and touch her face, but my hand lays powerless and unattached on the altar. She leans over and gently presses her lips to mine. Golden light fills the chamber. Her kiss saves me from oblivion.

The first thing I'm aware of is the cold. Next is the murmur of the crowd. For a moment, I think I'm on stage at an open-air festival in Oslo or Reykjavik, but then it all comes back to me.

I open my eyes and find that I'm encircled by a crowd of naked maniacs. They hiss and sing and press against one another. They drool like hungry jackals, or maybe it's venom that drips from their mouths.

I'm as naked as they are, kneeling with my hands bound to a pole behind me. The icy ground burns my shins and knees. The frigid air hurts my lungs.

Their leader approaches me. He's giving me the same con-artist smile he wears in every picture I've seen. His eyes are black vertical slits, set against swamp water.

He strokes my cheek. I try to pull away, but I'm bound too tightly. He laughs at my efforts to squirm free.

"Nathan Pharaoh, as I live and breathe." He presses his split tongue against his front teeth as he speaks the last word. It ends in a dragged-out hiss.

"Did you come here to find the truth that I shared with your Cleopatra? Did you come to hear the sermon that freed her heart and mind?"

I spit at him. His congregation jeers, but he laughs. It's an unnerving sound, like the rattle of a diamondback.

"You may not be able to appreciate it, but it was a beautiful gift that your daughter gave to your wife. To untether another from the yoke of existence—that is a joyous thing. It's a shame you weren't there to partake."

He brings his mouth close to my ear. His breath is hot on my face. It smells of rancid meat.

"I know you saw the aftermath ... photos of your wife's body, her face swollen and gray from the water she took on in the tub. Did you not find even a little beauty in that? Or in the way your daughter's face was painted in sickly yellow bruises radiating from the necrotic asp kiss on her cheek? I wonder if her dead, bulging eyes properly conveyed the anguish and ecstasy she felt in those final moments.

"Do you want to know the intimate details of that night? Exactly what transpired between your wife and daughter while you were playing Peter Pan on the other side of the world? The subtle flavors of pain they tasted before slipping into oblivion? I can tell you all of that if you like. I was there, in a sense."

I scream like a raging animal. I shout idle threats and violent boasts. The cult leader is unimpressed.

"Such delicious vitriol, Mr. Pharaoh. Your heart is heavy with it. There is no doubt you belong with us, maybe even more so than Cleo did."

His canine teeth extend, like those of a B-movie vampire. Venom drips from his mouth, dotting the packed snow with pin-pricks of blackness. The ground sizzles with each drop and dots of black nothingness mottle the ground. Tiny whirlpools of snow are siphoned into their gravity.

The cult leader's head sways hypnotically from side to side as he inches toward me, his jaw hyper-extended. I squirm like a rat on a glue trap, unable to break free from the ropes that tie my hands. I wait for his fangs to pierce my flesh and his venomous oblivion to flow through my being.

A scream echoes through the winter night. It's a visceral sound, saturated with pain. The cult leader snaps his terrible maw closed and turns toward the cry. I follow his gaze to the riotous mass of cultists behind him, but I can't see past them to identify what has them so panicked and enraged.

One of the zealots stumbles through the ranks of her brethren and into the arms of the cult leader. She holds the stump of her forearm in front of her face, staring at it with glazed eyes. Her skin is painted crimson by the bloody geyser pumping from her severed arm. The snow around them turns red, each drop bleeding more color into the white canvas of winter ground.

A spray of blood erupts from another of the maniacs, arching above the chaotic milieu. A third cultist hunches over and grabs at his stomach. He stumbles away from the pack and turns toward me. A clean slash nearly bisects him at the belly. He futilely tries to hold in his own viscera, but it oozes between his fingers.

The gutted cultist falls and I catch a glance at the source of the violence. Leo Schesmu, my old and ageless friend, stands at the center of the gathered cult, grinning and covered in gore. The blood-slicked blade of his meat cleaver gleams in the moonlight as he swings it in wide arcs, felling one member of the congregation after the other.

The last of the cultists crumples into a heap before Leo's blade. An ancient and forgotten epithet slips off their leader's forked tongue and he drops his dying devotee onto the frozen earth. He turns tail, but Leo is on his heels with the speed and grace of a cat. Leo's cleaver comes down on the venomous charlatan, cutting clear through his trapezius and lodging into his collar bone.

The evil bastard collapses and tries to slither away, but Leo stomps on his back and wiggles the cleaver free. I scream and cry, urging my friend on as he brings the blade down, over and over again. I watch in hysterical glee as he butchers my enemy.

When it's done—when the snake-eyed prophet lies lifeless and dismembered—Leo saunters toward me, running a bloody hand through his golden hair. He kneels in front of me and presses his forehead against mine.

"I told you that you were rubbish at violence, Nate."

I laugh and sob. Leo strokes my hair and plants a bloody kiss on my forehead before cutting me free.

"Do you feel any better?"

More than a dozen bodies scatter the ground, each flayed and dismembered. The immediate landscape is more red than white and the son of a bitch who whispered his toxic ideas into my daughter's ears lays dead before me. His corpse is barely recognizable as that of a man.

I survey the carnage and consider Leo's question. Do I feel better? Does his death ease the pain in my heart? Does the butchered wreckage of his body fill the void within me?

"No, Leo. I don't." My words are flat and lifeless.

Leo wraps his arms around me and I embrace him in kind. A snake crawls out from under the offal of the dead prophet.

My chin on Leo's shoulder, I watch as it slithers away, painting scarlet curves on the frozen ground in its wake.

JANUARY

The clock strikes midnight and I close my eyes to make a wish. The room erupts into a chorus of joyful screams. Guests break into pairs, exchanging drunken kisses. A few share their lips with several different people, laughing and smiling between each kiss. And then there are those who look for someone to pair up with but find no takers.

A few girls vie for my attention. Some shoot coy glances in my direction. One bites her lip and glares right at me. They're pretty, sexy even, but the thought of sharing a New Year's kiss with anyone but Dalia makes me sick to my stomach.

People are singing, out of tune and out of time, along with the bundled-up celebrities on the television. They slur sentiments about letting go of the past and embracing life anew as another year dawns. I sing along, out of habit I suppose, but the words are a lie, to me at least. Nothing feels new. Nothing feels different.

The front door opens and a man walks into the house. The girl clinging to his arm is crying, her eyes red and puffy. They are both dressed in white linen pants and a matching sweatshirt, but his face is hidden beneath the shadows of a voluminous hood. A sickle hangs loosely in his grip, its curved blade slick with blood. His clothes are stained with crimson splatters.

All eyes turn toward him and the mood immediately takes on a solemn tone. Rowdy voices hush. The din of a dozen simultaneous conversations retreats into a collection of whispers. Even the volume of the music seems to drop in his presence.

I can't gauge the temperature of the room. Are they afraid? In awe? Everyone watches him like they are waiting for something, but I'm not sure what.

The man in white pulls the girl at his side closer and kisses her on the head. He raises the sickle over his head and blood flows across the arc of the blade, then drips from the tip.

"Rebirth!"

The partygoers howl and hoot. "Rebirth!" they shout, just out of unison.

Is this another cult? Did I escape that lunatic den in the Colorado mountains just to end up in a small town of Kentuckian madmen?

It occurs to me how little I know of these people. The only one I've ever met is Beth Alrded. I knew her when she was a fashion model in LA, back when she dated Sebastian for a few months. I couldn't believe it when I saw her waiting tables at a diner in Kentucky, looking nearly as young as she had over a decade before. She's the one who invited me to this party, but I'm not even sure whose house this is.

My eyes dart from person to person, looking for visible expressions of madness—looking for reptilian eyes—looking for the cruel smile that came to dominate my daughter's expressions.

I'm pretty good at reading folks and I don't see any of that chaos or darkness in these people. I see no malice in their celebration. It does seem tainted with a subtle breed of melancholy, however.

Some of the party-goers express a sense of relief. Others seem joyous and offer thankful toasts. A few gently weep and accept the embrace of those nearby. Several people bring drinks to the couple dressed in white and give them tight, loving hugs.

Beth approaches me and offers a glass of white wine in a plastic champagne flute. I take it and thank her, but I find myself reluctant to drink more. She follows my gaze to the man with the sickle, then turns to me with a sad smile.

"Don't you mind all that. Just a local tradition. The new year is kind of a big deal here."

"Is that real blood?"

"It's not as scary as it looks."

"That's not an answer."

She shrugs and sits down beside me, then clinks her drink against mine.

"This town may not look like much, Nathan, but there's a certain kind of magic here. That L.A. lifestyle almost killed me, but I was able to start over here. Maybe you can as well."

"My family's gone, Beth. There is no starting over."

She takes my hand and squeezes it. I find myself wondering what kind of toll Los Angeles took on her. What did she lose in California, and what did she find in this lonely little slice of Americana just off the loneliest road?

"There's something you should see ... someone you should see."

Beth stands up and urges me off the couch. I let her lead me through the house, and past the couple clad in white. They are talking with an older woman, laughing and reminiscing about someone they lost. My pace slows as my eyes fall upon the bloody sickle hanging from the man's hand.

Beth gives my arm a tug and motions toward the front door. I follow her outside into the cold night. I pull out my cigarettes and offer her one. She declines. I guess she nixed some of her bad habits since her days in LA. I, however, light up and savor the taste and warmth of the cancerous smoke.

"Where are we going?"

"Look around. Tell me what you see."

I scan the street, looking for something notable. The houses are nothing special, save for the big yards and the generous spacing between the lots. Trees erupt from patches of dirt on the sidewalks at regular intervals, same as any small town in the States. The houses stop a few hundred yards down the road and give way to rows upon rows of corn.

"I see a John Denver song. Modest houses and big lots of land. Trees, grass, and corn."

Beth starts walking down the road, toward the cornfield. She motions for me to follow.

"And you don't see the magic in that?"

I shake my head and Beth laughs. She kneels and plucks a violet flower from a nearby bush. She twirls the stem between her fingers.

"Good God, Nathan, you are certainly a child of the Golden State."

I shrug, not understanding where she's going with all this. She holds the flower up to my face and smiles.

"It's mighty cold out, isn't it?"

I nod.

"Yet the flowers are in bloom, green leaves hang from the trees, and the corn stalks stand tall in the field. This town is alive, even in the season of death."

Beth smiles at me and I'm reminded of how unchanged she

looks. No, that's not quite right. She's changed. Her eyes hold less pain and her expressions are genuine. She's let go of the practiced, California artificiality that is expected from anyone who lives in the public eye.

So no, she's not unchanged, but rather unaged. There are no laugh lines around her eyes and no dark circles. Her hair is free of silver threads. Maybe it's clean living and fresh air. Maybe it's something more.

We walk to where the houses end and Beth leads me to the edge of the cornfield. She tells me to snub out my cigarette. I take one last drag and flick it into the street. Beth takes my hand and leads me in between the rows of corn.

The stalks are taller than us, healthy and full. There's a rich, earthy scent that undercuts the crisp smell of winter. I don't know anything about farming or agriculture, but that doesn't seem right. Shouldn't all of this have been harvested? Shouldn't the fields be barren until spring? Or is that just the ignorance of a rock-star city boy?

The soil feels soft beneath my boots. That, I know for sure, is not the way things should be. It's cold enough to see my breath—cold enough that the air stings my cheeks and my fingers are going numb. The earth should be frozen solid.

The neat rows of cornstalks give way to twisting, labyrinthine paths. It's not the neat and cultivated corn maze of a harvest season attraction. The pathways are inconsistently narrow and curve this way and that. Corn is trampled, creating gaps in the rows.

I follow Beth as she navigates the field. The deeper we get, the taller the corn grows and the richer the wholesome smells become. The scents overwhelm me—the smell of soil and honey overlaid with something green and floral. Beneath it all is the subtle stink of fertilizer. Not the chemical stuff, but pure, composted cow shit.

Beth leads me through a narrow break in the stalks and we enter a large clearing. An old man lays dead on the ground. He's dressed in the same white clothes as the man with the sickle, though his garments are much bloodier. The wound across his throat leaves his head nearly severed. His skin is pale as the moon in the sky.

The old man's blood seeps into the ground as the last of it drizzles from his wound. The soil drinks up his essence. Above the grizzly scene, a scarecrow looms, the moon shining on it like a spotlight. It is ugly and, in the truest sense of the word, it is awesome.

This is no shoddy burlap mannequin, tied to a post, but an idol crucified on a massive Ankh. Linen bandages wrap its body, the tattered edges flapping like streamers in the cold wind. The thing's arms are outstretched like Christ. One hand holds a crook, the other a sickle.

Its head is that of an eagle, adorned with a crown woven from corn husks and desiccated scraps of skin shed from snakes. Feathers stretch down the effigy's neck and shoulders. They almost blend in with the dirty linen that covers its human body.

The idol looks down its amber beak at me. Its eyes remind me of eclipsed suns—rings of radiant gold surrounding black shadows.

"What the hell am I looking at?" I ask.

Beth places her hand on my shoulder. She squeezes it gently.

"This is a place of rebirth, Nathan. It's a sacred spot that provides sustenance, both physical and spiritual. Here you can draw upon what you need and advocate for miracles, but it's also a place you must give back to, if not now, then later."

"Is that what happened to him?" I point to the corpse of the old man.

"He lived a longer and happier life than most people can ever imagine. And now he gives back, so that others may have their own miracles. He walked into death's arms with dignity."

Death is ugly, always and without exception. There is no dignity in bleeding out and shitting your pants. There's nothing romantic about oblivion. Nothing noble about leaving your loved ones behind.

"And how does one get a miracle?"

Beth leans against me and kisses my cheek. "Just ask," she whispers, then walks off into the corn. I'm left alone with the idol and the dead man.

I look up at the totemic creature and scream. I scream for my Dalia … for my Cleo. I beg the thing to give them back … to renew them the way it does this blip of a town. I promise to do whatever I must to have them back. I'll swear any oath or commit any crime. I'll spill every last drop of my blood into the soil.

The sickle falls from the totem's hand as if in response to my last statement. I retrieve the tool and gaze up at the eagle-headed figure.

"My blood? Is that what you want? Is that the price?"

The idol is silent and still. Its stoicism infuriates me.

"You can have all of it! Every red ounce! Just give them back!"

I hike up the sleeve of my jacket and place the crescent blade against my wrist. Scarlet wells up on either side of the steel as I press my flesh against the sharp edge. I let out a gasp as I rotate the sickle, extending the width of my wound.

I drop the curved blade to the ground and blood follows. Nocturnal beetles crawl up from the soil, hungry for the nutrients I'm spilling. They scramble in the dirt, competing with the thirsty soil for every drop.

Cold begins to set in, followed by weakness. I sit down and wait for something to happen, either my wife and daughter to come walking out from the rows of corn, or for oblivion to deliver me to them.

Light-headed, I fall to my side. The soil is warm despite the January chill as if it's teeming with chemical reactions and brimming with both life and decay. I never take my eyes off the eagle-headed scarecrow, even as the cosmos above us whirl like a slowing top.

The idol nods, or at least I think it does. The rows of corn part and form a path—an earthen avenue aglow with moonlight. I crawl along the ground, leaving red trails of life.

The path grades down steeper the further I go until I'm kneeling before a black, abyssal cavern. A cold wind, infinitely more frigid than the winter air, pulses from the hole. I imagine it as the icy breath of a terrible god.

I hear Dalia's voice echoing from within. Cleo calls out to me in the carefree tone she possessed as a little girl. I try to yell back to them, but I'm too weak. My words come out as whispers.

A dam of tears breaks and I collapse, sobbing into the cavern. I feel myself tumbling, but I don't hit the ground. I just keep falling until everything fades to black.

February

Something cold and hard digs into my back. Several somethings. I can't bring myself to sit up, or even open my eyes. I shift where I lie and roll on my side, only to feel dense protrusions digging into my ribs.

Cold radiates from the earth and the air. It seeps through my flesh, through my bones, and into my soul. I feel brittle on the inside as if everything at my core might shatter.

The deafening sound of rushing water echoes all around me. The noise presses against my temples like the jaws of a vice. I try to remember where I am and how I got here. Visions of cornstalks and blood come to mind. I recall the soil opening up while some great bird watched from above. It's all fuzzy and I can't piece it together. It's too loud to think.

I force my eyes open and I find myself on the banks of a stream, in some cavernous underworld. The bones of countless dead litter the soil. Discarded skulls grin at me with eyes full of dirt.

A large turtle lay trapped, caged within the half-buried ribs of some bigger animal. It nudges the bones with its wrinkled face, unable to break free.

Beyond the shore, the water rages—white foam against utter blackness. It reminds me of a stream of flowing television static. The current moves toward a massive pyramid that straddles the river. The epic tomb seems to give off its own light—a harsh neon glow. The façade is pristine, like how the pyramids must have looked when they were new—smooth, polished sandstone topped with a golden apex.

A set of stairs rises from the water into a grand entrance at the center of the pyramid. Statues line both sides of the steps—stern-looking men, carved from stone. They carry scepters for smiting enemies, and ankhs to ensure their own immortality. Their crowns mark them as kings, or at least I think they do. That's what pharaohs look like in museums and in movies.

This image of perfection flickers out. The pyramid now looks weathered and eroded—ravaged by time and neglect. The smooth stone is marred and chipped, covered in crude, neon graffiti.

Images of dead rock stars replace the statues of bygone kings. They're all there, carved in stone. Hank and Elvis. Jim and Jimmy. Sid, Kurt, and Lemmy.

The Pyramid flickers back and forth between these states. For a few moments, it is a picturesque image of monumental architecture. The next, it is a ruin, surrendered to entropy.

In both versions, the entryway at the top of the stairs is dark—a perfect, rectangular ink stain on the white stone. I don't know what awaits me inside, but I feel that's where I must go.

I look at the raging monochrome river and I know that I'm not powerful enough to fight the current. I fear it will sweep me beneath the pyramid or drag me under the water before I reach it.

My eyes fall upon the turtle again. I approach him and nudge the skeletal cage he's trapped in. It's firmly rooted in the ground. I raise my boot and bring the heel down on one of the ribs, over and over. It splinters eventually. The turtle does not seem afraid, so I break a second rib, then a third, freeing the animal.

"A favor for a favor?" I ask him.

The turtle doesn't respond, but he waddles over and waits at my feet. I reach down and grab him by the sides of his shell. It's softer than I expected—more like leather than bone.

We approach the river's edge and I wade into current. The water is even colder than the air and the earth. I can hardly breathe as it seeps the heat from my body, and I almost drop the turtle when the water hits my balls.

The current tugs and I let it carry me away. My body goes horizontal, and I am floating on my belly, holding onto the turtle. He is a strong enough swimmer to carry us both downstream. He rides the current, using its incredible pull to his advantage. He is never caught in its grip but rather seems the master of it.

I feel things bump against me beneath the surface. My mind conjures images of monsters. Razor-toothed eels. Lurking crocodiles. Serpentine mermaids. I imagine them watching me from the depths of the river—hungering for my grief and my blood.

No evil things attack me. The turtle delivers me to the steps of the pyramid without incident. I thank him. He accepts my thanks with silence and dives beneath the current of black water and white foam.

My clothes, heavy and wet, cling to my skin. I find myself shivering as I look up at these stairs that seem to rise forever. Each step upward is miserable. Water sloshes in my boots, and my body aches. My breath is white in the air, and I imagine each respiration as another fraction of my life and my will slipping away.

The dead kings change into fallen rockers, and back again as I struggle with my ascent.

I don't know how long it takes me, but I make it to the entrance of the pyramid. There is no light within, but voices beckon from inside. They are familiar. I hear people from my past—folks I've hurt and folks who've hurt me. Loudest among the voices is Cleo. She calls me. She taunts me.

"Come and get us, Daddy," she hisses.

I step forward into the dark.

An aura of light follows me through the dark corridor of the pyramid. It doesn't radiate far, but it allows me to see the floor in front of me and the walls beside me. The stonework is carved with hieroglyphs, but they don't depict kings, slaves, or gods. No, it is my likeness engraved on the pyramid walls. I touch the relief that spells out my life and I find myself overcome with vertigo.

Suddenly, I'm back in California. It's summer, and it's hotter than it has been all year. There is no air conditioning in my room, or anywhere in the house. The grass outside my window, that little patch of yard that's mine to play on, has turned brown from the drought.

I can hear my parents fighting in the kitchen. I don't know what the argument is about, and I can't make out individual words, but the tone of their voices and the volume of their yelling tells me all I need to know.

There's nowhere to go—no escape but the record player. I don't bother going through my albums. I only have a few at this point, so I drop the needle on what's sitting on the turntable. *X*

Offender by Blondie comes on the speakers. It's not my favorite track, but it doesn't matter. I close my eyes and allow myself to be carried away by the music. The rest of the world becomes inconsequential. No more concern about the homework I'm not doing. No more anxiety over the kid who threatened to kick my ass tomorrow. No more fighting parents.

When I open my eyes *X Offender* is still playing, but it's a messy version with shitty vocals. My fingers hurt, and I know I'm playing the song wrong, just as I'm sure that Krissy isn't hitting the right notes. The drummer, a Barrio kid named Alejandro, is playing a simple 4/4 beat without any of the high-hat work that makes the rhythm interesting. We sound like garbage, but we're all smiles.

That youthful bliss doesn't last. Krissy goes to a party the next month with some college guys she meets, and no one ever sees her again. Alejandro quits music and school to get a job and help support his younger siblings. I keep playing guitar and fall deeper into drugs and booze.

The world dilates. The music fades. I find myself back in the pyramid.

I follow the reliefs on the wall, each image cataloging a piece of my history. There is the sun setting over the ocean as I walk away, my old Ibanez slung over my back, out to play my first tour. I see my mother's corpse laid out, a procession of mourners lined up before her lifeless body.

The next image shows Kyle, our first drummer, dismembered upon a table. Two figures with the heads of some animal I can't identify stand over his corpse. Each holds a crimson-stained blade. I can tell by the tattoos on the figures that these are Sebastian and myself. This one is symbolic. We didn't murder Kyle, but I suppose we did contribute to his death. Neither one of us did a damn thing to help out when he started self-destructing. It was easier to write him off and replace him.

I see my first date with Dalia. Her hair is rendered the same color as the graven sun above us in the image. I reach out and press my first two fingers against the stone, and I'm once again transported to the past.

We're standing on the cliffs overlooking Half Moon Bay. The grass under our feet is a deep emerald, and the ocean past the cliffs is a rich blue, just slightly darker than the clear sky. Whitecaps form around dark rocks jutting out of the water. It's beautiful, incredibly so, but the natural wonder is lost on me. All I can see is her. Those golden curls, like spirals of sunlight. The striking contours of her cheeks. The way her shirt teases the barest glimpse of her chest. The rest of the world barely exists.

I had asked her to come out for a drink at The Rainbow, but she said she was done having dates at bars. She told me if I wanted to go out with her I'd have to come up with something more interesting. Her hand touches mine, and I find myself thinking that I picked the right spot.

I lean toward her and reach out to brush a lock of hair from her face. She brings her lips toward mine and we kiss for the first time. Our lips seem to match up perfectly, like they were made for each other. She teases me with her breath, denying me her tongue. A tiny giggle escapes from her mouth into mine, then she kisses me more deeply. She tastes like coffee and clove cigarettes and everything that is right with the world.

The sunlight fades, as does the sensation of kissing my wife again for the first time. I try to hold onto it. I reach for her hips, trying to keep her close, desperate not to lose her again, but she dissolves into nothing, along with the ocean, the cliffs, and the sky.

I touch the image of us again as if I'm hitting play on a touchscreen. Nothing happens. I remain in the dark tomb. The relief of that first date looks more weathered now. The colors are faded. The carvings aren't as sharp.

I run my hand along the graven image of my wife once more, then move on. The art on the wall depicts more and more of the ups and downs of my existence. Performances and scenes from music videos. The death of my old man. The birth of my daughter.

My eyes stop upon an image of Dalia holding Cleo, just after her birth. A serpent lays coiled at my wife's feet, its sinister eyes locked on my baby girl. It makes me wonder if the evil that overtook Cleo had always been there, waiting to manifest. What a terrible thought.

The tomb walls show my failures as a husband and a father. It's all there, carved in stone. My selfishness. My neglect. I was barely ever there. Dalia and Cleo are picking apples, and I'm playing in Germany. It's my daughter's first day of school, and I'm recording an album in New York. Dalia is singing our little girl to sleep, and I'm at a party in Mexico City.

The corridor comes to an end and I am met with a statue of a woman. It could be either my wife or my daughter, for they both looked so much alike. I know from the vacuous hate in those stone, serpentine eyes, that it's Cleo. Her body is carved from white stone mottled with black. It gives her a reptilian countenance.

Living serpents cling to the statue of my daughter. They coil around her, hissing at me and flicking their tongues. They urge me to touch my hand to the stone. They challenge and goad me. I wonder what it means that I can understand their language. Have they made their way into my heart, just as they had with Cleo?

The statue opens its mouth and emits a terrible sound, like the creaking of breaking ice. My daughter's voice calls out to me, hateful and taunting.

"Do you have the balls to find out how it happened, Daddy?" it asks. "Are you man enough to see what you weren't there to stop?"

I don't want to see what she offers to show me. There are some things too terrible to face. I turn around, but there's nothing there. Not the corridor, not the wall, not even darkness. There is just this impossible nothing that is almost maddening to look upon.

"There's no going back, Nathan Pharaoh." The words are hissed in the language of snakes.

I close my eyes to the nothing and music begins to play. I can't tell if it's real, or just in my head, but does it matter? I hear Sebastian's voice, singing words that I wrote while I was in rehab.

Gotta walk through the darkness to get to the dawn
Gotta face those demons and all that's gone wrong
I will stare down the devil, I won't agonize
If it means I get one more glimpse of those blue eyes

I turn around and lock eyes with the idol of my daughter. The serpents coiled around her writhe and hiss. I reach out my hand and the statue does the same. Our fingertips meet and I am brought to the moment when my world came to an end.

MARCH

I wake up in a pile of blankets in a room that that I don't recognize. I'm naked, My heart pounding and I'm covered in sweat. I had the nightmare again. The same one I've had since my vision at the pyramid. The same one that has plagued me since I touched the statue of Cleo in that fever dream, if it was a dream. It has followed me from motel room to motel room—from friends' couches to strangers' beds.

I don't know where I am, but the room is laid out in an odd manner. The ceiling and the walls are painted white. It's dimly lit. Sheer curtains and scarves hang from criss-crossing clotheslines running along the ceiling. They form forming a maze of partitions. I stand up and push through the hanging panels of cloth—purple lace, cream-colored linen, and burgundy voile.

There are other people asleep in the room, men and women all about the floor, nude, passed out in heaps of blankets. One of the women looks familiar. Images of drinking with her flash through my mind, followed by vague memories of hollow sex. She's pretty, but she's missing something on the inside. You can almost see the longing within her—some terrible emptiness yearning to be filled. Maybe that's what drew us to each other.

Everyone is sleeping hard, almost as if they are drugged, but I don't see any paraphernalia strewn about, and everyone looks

63

healthy. These aren't addicts. It looks more like the aftermath of an orgy than a drug party. It makes me wonder if I was with anyone else last night.

The entryway to the room is double-width. There are no doors, just more sheer fabric hanging as a barrier. There is no break in the panel, so I stumble through it, clumsily, into the next room.

It's even stranger in here than in the last room. The only piece of furniture is an old Lazyboy. The brown leather is cracked and pale yellow stuffing can be seen beneath. In front of the chair is a wall made of cathode ray TVs. It's put together like a fieldstone wall, all different-sized televisions stacked floor to ceiling, none of them quite straight. The gaps are stuffed with VHS tapes, remote controls, and yellowing issues of TV Guide going back to the '50s.

Strange visions fill each screen. Some are disturbing vignettes of non-sequitur horror. Feral dogs with the faces of men. A procession of children carrying a tiny coffin through a playground. Moments of lust and sex morphing into violent murder. Other screens show images more fantastic and far less dreadful. Technicolor skies over fields of neon flora. A go-go club where mermaids dance in tanks above the dance floor. Sensual images of a plain-looking woman, writhing in sublime submission beneath a naked Christ.

I step further into the room, past the leather chair, and find a bearded man seated in it. He's naked, save for a pair of oversized sunglasses. He has a dwarfish frame, and his legs dangle off the edge, coming nowhere near the floor. His proportions are strange, not quite like anything I've seen on a person of any size. His feet are nearly as long as his calves, and his flaccid cock hangs down past his feet.

There are knobs, dials, and toggle switches coming up from the armrests on either side of the chair. The man in the chair fiddles with the controls, the movements of his fingers slow and deliberate.

"The dead king has risen," he says, then turns to me with a grin. His smile fades as he looks me up and down. "Well, not yet I suppose."

"Where am I? What is this place?"

"Me casa es su casa," he says.

"And you are?"

"I've had a lot of names, but you can call me Bes."

"Quite the setup you've got there, Bes." I say, pointing toward the wall of televisions. "Got some real 1980s supervillain vibes going on."

"We all play the villain from time to time, Nathan Pharaoh, but I assure you, there's nothing malicious happening here."

His attention returns to the TVs. He continues messing with the dials and knobs. I notice that the visions on the screens change as he does so. Sometimes it's a subtle difference—a change of hair color or one landscape slowly eroding into another. Other times it is startling and abrupt like a child's smile shifting into a mouthful of obsidian daggers.

"So what is happening?"

"I'm just showing people what they need to see. It's easier for some folks than others. Life's unfair.'

"And what do I need to see?"

Bes looks at me. The corners of his mouth turn downward. I get the impression there is a sadness in his eyes, behind those massive goggles.

"The worst thing, I'm afraid."

"I've already seen the worst thing," I tell him.

"No, you've been shown the worst thing. You haven't allowed yourself to see it, however. Not really."

I look at the images flickering across the multitude of screens. Dreams and nightmares. Distorted memories. Past traumas, grown into colossi.

"Why should I allow myself to see it, Bes? What good can come from staring tragedy in the face? How much more pain am I expected to shoulder?"

"You're going through Hell, Pharaoh, I know. The only way out is to keep going."

Bes turns the knobs and flips the switches on the arm of his chair. The visions played out on the screens dissolve into static. One by one, new images come to life across each television. They form a fluid mural—a film playing across the wall of TVs as if it were a movie screen. My daughter's face comes into focus, and my heart stutters.

Dalia opens the front door to find Cleo standing beyond the threshold. Her face is too gaunt and her body disturbingly thin. Once her eyes were filled with light and life. Now they are cold, reptilian slits. Hard living and neglect have robbed her of youth, in both body and soul.

Tears run down Dalia's cheeks and she chokes back a sob. Someone else might not know if she's crying out of sorrow or relief. It's both of course. She is relieved to see our daughter alive, but heartbroken by how harshly the world has treated her—how harshly Cleo has allowed the world to treat her.

I can't see any of myself in Cleo. She looks so much like her mother they could almost be twins. Sadly, Cleo looks like the older of the two. Her hair is ratty and dried out. Dalia has some laugh lines, and a few creases where her lips meet, but her complexion is otherwise flawless. Cleo's face is a roadmap of wrinkles and pockmarks, aging her far beyond her years.

Dalia ushers our daughter into the house. They talk briefly, but Dalia can see how tired Cleo is. She urges her to take a shower, telling her they can talk later. Cleo does so without much of an argument.

Dalia fills the kettle and places it on the stove. She pulls down a tea box and lays out a selection of flavors. It's been so long since she's seen our daughter that she doesn't even know what she drinks. I wouldn't have known either. The only reason I know now is because of the rose mint tea bag I found in the half-empty cup when I got home from Europe. Dalia never drank rose mint.

Cleo comes back downstairs. Her hair is damp and slicked back. It looks darker than it should. Maybe it's just that it's wet. Maybe it's the lighting. Maybe something else.

She's wearing a threadbare pair of jeans and a t-shirt with an inverted ankh. Her feet are bare and her toenails are lacquered in chipped paint, the same green as her fingernails.

Dalia is trying to talk to her, but she doesn't know what to say. She doesn't know our daughter anymore, so she focuses on immediate things.

"How are you feeling?"

"I hope you know that you can stay as long as you like."

"I wish your father was here. He'd be so happy to see you."

I wish I'd been there too. Would things have been different? Would my wife and daughter still be walking and breathing? Would I have been able to save them? Would I have been able to save myself, or would I be dead too? Proper dead, I mean, not just in my heart and soul.

Dalia steps off-screen, stage left, but I can still hear her voice. She is trying her best to keep the conversation going without grilling our daughter about where she's been, what she's been doing, or who she's been doing it with.

Cleo reaches into her pocket and pulls out a plastic baggie. It looks like a gram of coke, but I know that's not what it is. She reaches across the table and dumps the white powder into her mother's Earl Grey. She swirls the tea bag in the cup to mix in the drug before Dalia can notice.

Dalia comes back into frame. I beg the dwarf to pause the video. I don't want to see what comes next. I just want to look at my wife's face—the way she purses her lips—lips that I'll never kiss again—the look of love and concern in her eyes. I just want to stare at her and do nothing else until hunger, exposure, or heartbreak claim my life.

The video doesn't pause. It keeps playing and I see Dalia take a sip from the mug. I'm mumbling, begging her not to drink. The mumbling turns to blubbering and I feel my eyes well with tears.

Dalia and Cleo keep talking, but Dalia starts to slur her words after a few minutes. She gets drowsy and confused. Cleo tells her she needs a hot bath and some wine. Dalia protests but Cleo hushes her. She takes her mother's hand and leads her upstairs.

The screen goes to commercial. I see Sebastian dry-humping a mic stand and one of my songs plays from the speakers. Jimmy is pounding away on a drum kit in the background. And of course, I'm there on the stage. I'm there, playing fucking guitar and smiling like the world isn't ending.

Tour dates scroll up the screen.

8-11 – Puskas Arena, Budapest
8-12 – National Arena, Bucharest
8-14 – LaDefense, Paris

I keep watching, shaking my head as the dates scroll further. I shut my eyes and sob. When I open them, the dates are closer to the one I dread seeing.

8-21 – Circo Massimo, Rome
8-23 – Deutsch Bank Park, Frankfurt
8-25 – Hyde Park, London

I feel my stomach tighten as the dates scroll. I feel and taste bile as it rises in my throat. My hands tremble and my knees feel as if they will give out any second.

8-27 – Bellahouston Park, Glasgow
8-28 – Telenor Arena, Oslo

I've been reading the dates in threes, but these are the last ones. We never played again after the 28th, because that's the day the world ended. Mine at least.

And where was I? Grinning and strutting around playing rock star.

Where was I? Not home. Not keeping Dalia safe. Not keeping Cleo safe.

Where was I? Out on the road, with my pack of lost boys, enjoying my eternal childhood, while life ended for the people I loved the most.

The commercial ends, then flashes back to my home. Dalia is in the oversized tub in the master bathroom. Her eyes are barely open. She tries to talk, but the sounds she makes are incoherent whispers. Cleo is stroking her hair, shushing her.

I don't know if she's awake when our daughter nudges her mother's head beneath the water. I can't tell if the way she's thrashing beneath the water is a conscious fight for breath and life, or an involuntary action from her panicked, primal brain. I hope she wasn't awake for it. I hope there was no pain, and that she didn't know it was our daughter who was killing her.

The drowning takes longer than I expected—longer than anyone should have to suffer. Cleo doesn't say a word as she murders her mother. The only sound comes from Dalia thrashing in the water. It reminds me of some comic about Jack the Ripper that I read in my twenties. There was this section of Jack butchering a victim, and it went on for pages and pages with no dialogue. Just panel after panel of silent violence. This isn't bloody in the same way as the comic, but it's real and it's worse.

Dalia's movements slow. The sound of sloshing bathwater quiets. Cleo relaxes and sits on the floor beside the tub. Her breathing is a soft, rhythmic hiss.

Nothing happens for several more minutes. Cleo stays seated on the tile, her jeans wicking up the water that splashed out of the tub. Her body is so slight that it's hard to see her draw breath, but I can hear it. It's the only sound.

Finally, she stands up. She strips out of her t-shirt and her wet jeans. She's wearing nothing underneath. Her body is haggard, older than her years, same as her face. Her ribs protrude tight beneath her skin. She's covered in tiny scars— the ghosts of razor blade kisses and cigarette burns. I know that many are self-inflicted, but I wonder how many came from sadistic lovers.

It doesn't matter where the scars came from. Ultimately, the fault lies with Dalia and me. Those are the marks of having an absentee father, more loyal to music and the road than to his family. They are the scars of negligence, left by a mother who couldn't see her daughter's pain, right in front of her eyes. We thought that she'd have a perfect life. Endless money. Big house. Ponies and nice clothes and everything a girl could want. Everything except for a mom and dad who were present.

Cleo reaches into her purse, which sits on the back of the toilet. It's a big, faux leather bag with a tarnished chain strap. She reaches in and produces a cotton sack. Something is writhing inside it.

Cleo opens the drawstring and pulls out a brown snake, dotted with a pattern of black dots. I don't know much about snakes or reptiles, but the thing looks evil to me. It coils around her arm. She smiles and coos at it as if it were a puppy.

She steps into the hot tub and sits down beside her dead mother. There's a song on her lips. I don't recognize the tune, but I know it will haunt me for the rest of my days.

She lets herself slip beneath the water's surface and pulls the snake under with her. The camera follows her beneath the water. For a moment, the screen is obscured by bubbles, but it clears up and I can see Cleo in profile. Here hair floats around her like a halo of seaweed.

The snake wrapped around her arm wriggles and panics. She grips it by the neck and brings it toward her face. Her lips part as if she's waiting for a lover's kiss. The serpent strikes her, first biting her lip, then snapping at her face several times. Tiny plumes of pink blood begin to cloud the water.

Cleo keeps hold of the snake. It bites her several more times before she relinquishes her grasp. A smile crosses her face and her eyes roll back as if she's in ecstasy. The serpent slithers up her naked body, escaping the tub and defying death.

The TV shuts off with a click. I stand stunned and unmoving, save for the trembling that wracks my body—silent save for the sobs that echo from deep within my chest.

I turn to the dwarf. I ask why he would show me this. I ask what I have done to deserve having such sights thrust upon me.

"Maat," he replies.

"Matt?" I ask in response.

"Maat. Truth and justice."

"You're to be judged, Nathan Pharaoh. You should know the facts of your case before you face the scales of justice."

"And who is it that will judge me?"

"The only one who can."

APRIL

It's been about six weeks since my encounter with the dwarf. I don't think I've ever drank this much, even in the days right after losing Cleo and Dalia. I keep hoping my liver will give out. Each day when I wake up, I check my eyes for jaundice, but there's never any yellow. Not yet at least.

Six weeks of recurring nightmares. Six weeks with the morbid visions of my family's last moments playing on loop in my head. I don't know how much longer I can live with it. I'm not sure of today's date, but I know April's coming to a close. I'd hoped I wouldn't live to see May.

The road is twisting before me—an endless serpent tail preserved in asphalt. The curves of the highway seem to sway and change shape as I drive. I can feel the ground shifting beneath my tires, like the contracting muscles of some great beast. Or maybe I'm just too drunk.

Probably I'm not drunk enough. I can still feel and think. Still drone on to myself in this endless internal monologue. Still see the horrendous last moments of my daughter and wife, forced upon me in nightmares and visions.

I take another swig from my can. Maybe I should stop at the next gas station and get something stronger. Beer just isn't cutting it.

As I turn the wheel and follow the contours of the winding

road, my headlights shine into the darkness. I catch glimpses of vermin and monsters skittering away from my high beams. Rats. Wild dogs. Shambling meth heads.

I wonder what would happen if I drove off the road. What would happen if I turned off the headlights? Would the things from the dark descend on me? Would the rats burrow into my flesh? Would the dogs tear me to bits? Maybe, but it's the dead-eyed addicts I find the most frightening. If my Cleo would kill her own mother for no discernible reason, what would these men—if you could call them that—what would they do to me for a few bucks and a '56 Les Paul?

Maybe I'd be better off. I ponder the idea—play it out in my head as I finish my fourth or fifth beer. Who's counting? Even if every vile thing hiding on the blackened edges of Route 50 came at me, biting, ripping, raping, it would be a quicker death than the slow demise I've been courting.

The orange pyramid of a Citgo station glows like a beacon down the road. I follow the light and pull into the filling station. The pumps are all free and the lot is empty save for an old Triumph bike.

I park the car in front of one of the pumps and head into the station. There is little light between the pumps and the door to the station's market. All through this road trip, I've been afraid to step out of the light. I remember feeling like my headlamps were the only thing keeping the evil things at the fringes of the world at bay. Now I just don't give a shit. Let them come for me.

I stride forward, through the darkness and find myself unmolested. I can feel them around me—vermin, spirits, monsters—but they scuttle away at my approach. I hear their panicked shambling and skittering. Part of me wonders why they fear me. What am I but a washed-up drunk who was too weak to keep his family safe? I don't care enough to give it more than a passing thought, however. The monsters don't matter. The only spirits I'm concerned about are in a bottle.

The door issues a jarring, electronic chime as I walk into the mini-mart. There's a biker behind the counter, leaning back in a chair with his boots on the counter. He's got long black hair and skin the color of rust. His cowboy hat has a weird little animal skull on it, and the brim covers his eyes. I swear I've seen him somewhere before but hell if I can remember right now.

I stagger to the counter, pulling out my wallet. I tell him to put forty dollars on the pump and ask him where he keeps the strong stuff.

"Hello, Nathan Pharaoh," he says, without looking up.

"I thought you looked familiar. Can't quite place where we met."

The biker tips his hat upward and glares at me with reptilian eyes. I'm almost unphased at this point. Everywhere I go there's some bitch or bastard staring at me with that serpentine glare. It's almost mundane at this point. Evil and entropy are the new normal. Maybe they always have been and I just hadn't noticed before.

"Can we even say we met? A version of you crossed paths with a version of me back in the desert. But I don't think either of us is the same man we were then."

"That's pretty deep."

The biker laughs. There is nothing pleasant in the sound.

"Neither one of us is deep, Nathan Pharaoh. We aren't even shallow."

I look past him at the hard liquor behind the counter. I'm

bored with bizarre strangers saying weird shit to me.

"I'll take a bottle of Jack."

"I stole that line from Nietzsche. He said it about women, but I think it fits better for men like us."

I slap my money on the counter and keep my mouth shut. I don't want to entertain any further bullshit. I just want to be wasted.

"Old Friedrich also said something about hunting monsters and staring into abysses. I think that might apply to us as well. Don't you think?"

"Jack Daniels," I say the words slow and firm. "Forty on the pump."

The biker smirks at me. Just like his laugh held no mirth, his smile is a dead and joyless thing. He turns and grabs the bottle of whiskey, then rings me up.

I grab my booze and head for the door. A chorus of voices calls out. Cleo's voice. The cult leader who poisoned her mind. The biker's voice and my own. All of us at once.

"This man was once my enemy, but I crawled inside him and took all that he was. Just like I did to your daughter."

My reflection glares at me from the picture window at the front of the mini-mart. It's an imperfect doppelganger— ghostly and tinged in dark tones. Its pupils are reptilian slits. Like the biker's eyes. Like the bartender at Old Ironsides back in September. Like my daughter.

"I've done the same to you. You just don't see it yet. But you will."

I watch my reflection's mouth move even as I clench my jaw and grind my teeth. I hear its words while I stand silent.

Enraged, I rush at the window and swing my bottle of Jack Daniels at the glass. I want to shatter the window and watch the monstrous simulacrum break into a million tiny pieces. That's not what happens.

Instead, my hand passes through the glass, as easily as it would the surface of a lake. The me on the other side takes hold of my wrist. It swings me around, pulling me into the looking glass, so to speak. I'm drunk, unsteady, and caught off guard, so I offer no resistance. I tumble to the ground and the bottle skitters from my hand. I look up just in time to watch my evil twin pick up the bottle of whiskey and step through the glass and into the real world.

I try to stand but stumble and fall face down. Slurred curses drip like drool from my mouth as I stumble to find my footing. The other Nathan watches from beyond the glass. His laughter and smile are as unsettling and as joyless as those of the biker.

I stagger forward and throw myself against the glass. It doesn't give. I can neither break it nor can I pass through. The doppelganger raises one eyebrow and gives me a salute before walking away, leaving me trapped in the phantom realm of the window's reflection.

My vision is a horizontal slit. I can see my evil self, or enough of his face at least to tell that it's him. His eyes are fixated on something straight ahead, but he occasionally glances my way. It takes me a moment to realize that I'm looking through the other side of a rearview mirror.

I'm watching him drive my car. I can see the road through the back window—highway lines popping into existence under the illumination of the Lincoln's taillights, then vanishing into the darkness.

"They say that it's darkest before the dawn, Pharaoh. I say that's bullshit. There is no sunrise coming. There are no better days at the end of this road."

He still speaks in a choir of voices, but there is a hiss beneath it all. It's an inhuman sound resonating below his words.

"There can be no dawn for you because I devoured your sun. And you ... well, you just don't burn brightly enough to bring the day on your own."

He takes both hands off the wheel and opens the bottle of Jack. I see the highway lines begin to drift to the right. He pays no mind to the swerving of the car.

"This old boat doesn't have the best alignment, huh?"

I want to reach through the mirror and grab him. I want to strangle and beat him and let the car careen off the road while we battle across the front seats. I can't escape my prison on the wrong side of the mirror though, so I'm stuck just watching him.

"What are you?" I ask. The thought never occurred to me before. This vile thing that crawled inside my daughter's soul and the souls of so many others must have a name. It must have a will and a purpose.

"I am the degradation of something into nothing and I am nothing given form. I'm the void that came before Ptah, or Enki, or God Almighty. I am the word of creation spoken backward and the black hole in your heart."

He presses the bottle of Jack to his lips and takes a swallow. I feel the burn of the whiskey as it passes down his throat. He pulls the bottle away from his mouth and lets out a raucous holler.

"I wonder how fast this old gas guzzler can go. You ever try to push the needle?"

My doppelganger places one hand on the wheel and straightens the trajectory of the car. I hear the growl of the engine grow louder as he presses down on the gas. The broken lines on the road behind us begin to strobe faster and faster.

I find myself getting motion-sick as he takes the curves of the winding road at increasing speeds. The tires screech every now and then, and I wonder how long it will take him to spin out at this speed. The Lincoln wasn't built for this.

"Entropy is the natural state of things. Existence was a mistake. That's why it breaks down. Why things die. Why civilizations collapse. None of this was meant to be. Decay is the universe righting itself into non-existence. I am the steward of that decay."

He nudges the wheel and glides into the wrong lane. The piercing cry of a car horn shrieks out over the roar of the engine. Headlights fill the cabin of the car. The other me doesn't flinch. He makes no move to pull back into the right lane.

I hear the shriek of tires and the oncoming headlights vanish. A moment later I see the other car in our rearview. It's swerving wildly, having just avoided us. I pray for it to regain control, but it spins out to the side and slams into a pole. The other me smiles.

"It's ironic, right? We're still here, intact and whole because I have no fear of annihilation … because I embrace it. But that man or woman … hell maybe it was a whole family … they're probably dead because they were so desperate to cling to this miserable existence."

I slam my fists against … I'm not sure what. I'm not even sure where I am or what barrier holds me back. Existence on the other side of the mirror is nebulous. It's a nonsense thing. Yet that's where I am.

"Even you, Nathan Pharaoh ... after all you've been through ... after all you've lost, you're too scared to eat a bullet or drink some Drano. Well, let me help you, just like I helped our dear Cleopatra."

Hearing him utter my daughter's name makes me sick. I scream and cry in impotent rage.

The other me takes another swig of whiskey and then leans back with his hands above his head. I feel the car swerving toward the side of the road. I hear the rumble strips, then the hard drop as we drive off the shoulder. The car careens forward, the suspension bouncing over the uneven ground.

"Goodbye, Nathan Pharaoh."

Those are the last words I hear before the car comes to a violent stop, accompanied by the whine of bending steel and the tinkling rain of shattered glass. My consciousness, or my soul, or whatever was stuck behind the other side of the mirror, shoots out through the rearview and into the real world. I find myself in the driver's seat, bloody, broken, and in incredible pain.

I look out through the shattered windshield. It's dark and I can barely make out the front end of my car wrapped around a tree. The headlights flicker and dim. Monsters skitter forth from the surrounding darkness. I can hear their hungry growls and insane jabbering.

The rearview mirror now sits on the passenger seat in a heap of glass. I look into the cracked mirror and the other me looks back. As my consciousness fades, I realize that he was right. The serpent was in me long before it was in Cleo. I was the void in my daughter's childhood— a ghost, rarely found outside of records and music videos. I was the degradation of something into nothing and now I am nothing given form.

MAY

Lights. Pain. Voices. It's all a blur. I hear men and women with severity in their voices, shouting things I don't understand. Lights shine from above, blinding me. They strobe in and out, or maybe it's my vision that's faltering—a sporadic blindness ushering me to the end, like the lights flicking off and on at closing time

The pain stands out above the other sensations. It is profound. The physical suffering brings a sort of symmetry to my being at least—the agony of my body now mirrors that of my soul.

I feel a sense of movement. It's a smooth feeling, like floating, rather than being carried. I imagine that I'm lying on a raft, drifting downriver. That would be a pleasant way to go—to drift along the water and fade away.

My trajectory turns sharply, and I'm jerked away from my daydream of a river to oblivion. A man yells some sort of gibberish. The voices all sound so serious … so concerned.

"What's there to be concerned about?" I try to ask. The words come out as mumbled nonsense.

A figure leans over me. All I can make out is a featureless silhouette against the glaring lights above.

"Try and relax, Mr. Pharaoh," the figure says. It is the first thing I've understood. "We're doing everything we can to help."

I try to ask him what he means. I try to ask where I am and what kind of help they think I need. The words are caught in my chest. Unable to speak, I close my eyes and heed the man's advice. It's a difficult task, however, to relax while agony radiates through your every nerve. The intimacy I've shared with mental pain has prepared me at least a bit for this, however. Heartache and physical trauma are not quite the same monster, but they are cousins of sorts.

One of the interesting things about intense suffering is that one can ride it like a high. That's not to say it's pleasant, but it pulls you out of the mundane and buffers one from the rest of existence. I give myself to the pain and let it take me.

There's a strange breed of relief in this. Guilt and sorrow are washed away. I feel no yearning for what I've lost. All there is is this new suffering, which is preferable to the agony of the soul.

I've stopped moving. The men and women are shouting. I feel a pinch in my arm, then the sensation of something cold entering my veins. The pain begins to fade. I try to scream for them to stop. I silently urge them not to numb my body, because the pain is the only thing that keeps back the emotional suffering. Only drool and nonsense come from my lips.

My muscles go limp. My eyelids fall closed. Fade to black.

The serpent whispers in my ear, because oblivion is its home, and silence is its language. It doesn't taunt or mock. Those unwords that it speaks are soothing. I begin to understand why Cleo was drawn to it.

I relax as it coils around my heart.

For a while there is nothing. Perfect, merciful oblivion. It may be minutes or eons. I can't tell, nor does it matter.

I moan and curse as self-awareness washes over me again.

My eyes flutter open and I find myself in a dimly lit chamber. A monstrous figure stands over me, with the body of a man and the head of a dog.

The hybrid leans over my chest with a small obsidian blade poised in one hand. He draws the edge along the left side of my torso. The blade is so sharp that I barely feel the cut. The same can not be said as he plunges his hand into the incision and grabs at my insides.

I squirm and scream as the dog-headed man draws my intestines out. He's like a grisly magician pulling out a neverending stream of bloody handkerchiefs. He discards my guts and continues to root inside me. I feel him grip my liver, my spleen, my appendix. He rips each away from blood vessels, or cartilage, or whatever the hell moors them in place.

Lungs. Glands. Stomach. He removes each with a cool disinterest, placing them aside. Only when he tears out my heart is there a moment of pause. He holds it aloft and studies it. It's still beating in his hand. Black veins snake around the organ. They seem to slither about.

The jackal-headed thing walks away with my heart. It approaches an old-timey balancing scale, the kind on the cover of Metallica's *And Justice for All*. This one is more ornate—a masterful piece of art, crafted from pure gold. Even the chains that hold the plates are fashioned out of fine and delicate gold.

One plate is empty. A white feather sits upon the other. When I say white, I don't know that I'm doing it justice. It is the purest white I've ever seen, so much so that it hurts to look upon. If you can imagine the deepest part of the galaxy, someplace where light has never dared touch, the color of this feather would be the opposite of the blackness that would lurk in such a place.

Couch Surfing Through the 12 Chambers of Hell

Huddled near the scales, I see the ghosts of dead kings. Elvis and Hank the first. Cliff and Randy. Johnny's there, dressed in all black, next to Buddy in his signature glasses. Pete and Joey stand behind the others, towering above them. Long black hair frames their faces like cloaks. Their leather jackets are worn and weathered like ancient armor.

The hybrid approaches the scale with my heart. It holds it above the empty plate.

Whispers drift from the mouths of the dead kings. They tell me that there's magic that can still save me. Songs can be sung to sway the balance in my favor. Words of beauty can be uttered that can outshine any sin.

I realize now that this is my moment of judgment. I have no interest in cheating or charming my way out of damnation. No clever bit of lyrical wordplay can undo my selfishness or neglect. No melody can be so beautiful as to make up for my failures. Let the dead kings keep their magic. I'm done hiding my cowardice behind raging guitars and my lack of worth behind stave and bar.

The jackal wouldn't be tricked either way. The scars on its body are identical to mine. Tattoos mark its skin, mirror images of my own. An ankh on its wrist. A barbed wire web on its elbow. The name *Cleo* on the side of its neck. Its face is that of a dog, but behind those canine features, I can see my own eyes.

The conversation I had with Bes the Dwarf back in March echoes in my mind.

And who is it that will judge me?

The only one who can.

The dead kings urge me to use music and magic to weigh the scales in my favor. I lay silently as my jackal-headed doppelganger places my heart upon the scale. The plate beneath it plunges down with the weight of my every failure and sin.

"Nathan Pharaoh," the hybrid says in my own voice. "You have been found lacking. Ammit approaches."

A terrible growl echoes from the darkest reaches of the cavern. It's the sound of extinction at the hands of falling meteors. It's the noise of tsunamis crashing upon cities and the grinding of steel and stone being dragged into the sea.

The ghosts of the dead kings vanish at the sound. For all their bluster and ego, they scatter like frightened children at the coming of oblivion. I suppose that's all they have left to fear. Deep down they all know that even ghosts die and that no legacy is eternal.

I watch as the jackal-headed judge retreats to the shadows and a beast comes into view. It is massive, easily the size of a bus and the cavern shakes with each step it takes.

The monster is a hybrid as well, but with no human aspects. Rather, it's a chimeric thing—a crocodile-headed beast with the mane and forequarters of a lion, but the back side of a hippo. It moves toward me with a grace that is at odds with its monstrous size and appearance.

The scale sways and shakes with each step the monster takes. My heart is still dragging down the plate beneath it with its terrible weight. Black, serpentine veins writhe beneath its chambers and ventricles—the serpent celebrating my damnation.

I can feel the monster's hot breath. I can hear the hunger in its growl and in the dripping splashes of drool from its watering mouth. There are only seconds left, and then everything ends. No more pain. No more guilt. No more missing my girls.

Eyes closed, I call images of Cleo and Dalia into my mind. I see them as I did in the good times. I can hear Cleo's tiny voice calling for me as I drop my bags in the foyer after months on tour. I can feel her tiny arms wrap around my waist and the softness of her hair as I pat her head.

I hear Dalia's voice in my ear, whispering that she missed me. I can feel her body and her lips, showing me the same sentiment later in the night.

Each of those little moments is a crystalized bit of my daughter and my wife. Those memories exist only in my mind. I panic, realizing that when I'm gone, those moments will disappear with me. It's like I'm about to let them die all over again.

I open my eyes and call for the dead kings. I implore them to give me their spells or songs, or whatever magic might stave off oblivion. It's too late. The monster's slobber drips upon my flesh. Seconds pass, just enough for me to be consumed by one last moment of pain and regret, and then the beast is upon me.

I'm pinned in place by paws like tree stumps and dagger-like claws. Jagged teeth tear at my flesh. My bones crack and crunch beneath jaws of incredible size and impossible strength.

There's no fighting the beast. I can't move beneath its weight or speak through the pain it inflicts. Even if I had the strength to fight, I lack the brawn to fell such a monster. They say music soothes the savage beast. I try to sing or hum or make any noise that might be construed as melodic. All that comes out is a hollow rattle.

My last thoughts before darkness sets in are of Cleo and Dalia, and how in my final moment, I've failed them once more.

JUNE

Beep Beep Beep Beep
...
Beep Beep Beep Beep
...
Beep Beep Beep Beep
Pssshhhh woo click click
Beep Beep Beep Beep
Pssshhhh woo click click
Beep Beep Beep Beep
Pssshhhh woo click click

A rhythm wakes me from the void of nonexistence. That rhythm is all there is. Just a simple song, floating through oblivion.

Beep Beep Beep Beep
Pssshhhh woo click click

There's not much to it. Real minimalist, industrial kind of vibes. There's often beauty in such simplicity, though.

The rhythm comes in short beats, each succinctly cut off. It's as if the void which surrounds me seeks to silence the sound. It's like it sees an aspect of flame in the song as if it might grow out of control if not snuffed out.

I hear the serpent hissing in my ear. It's telling me to ignore the music. It's urging me back into the black, but I miss music.

Couch Surfing Through the 12 Chambers of Hell

I miss rhythm and melody. I miss joy and dance.

It hisses again, trying to shush my thoughts and to drown out the music. The rhythm is locked in my mind though.

Beep Beep Beep Beep

Pssshhhh woo click click

I tap my finger in time with the beeps, suddenly aware of my body. There's a pain in my hand with each movement, but it's not overwhelming. It's welcome in fact. How long has it been since I've felt anything?

A hairline fracture streaks across the nothingness above me—a lightning bolt fissure. The tiniest bit of light seeps through the crack. The void howls with anger and hate.

"Oh shit, he's moving!"

I'd know that voice anywhere. That voice turned my poems into songs. It danced and floated over my chord progressions and harmonized with melodies I drew out from the aether. It helped turn a poor kid into a rich man.

"Sebastian."

The name crawls from my lips as a dry whisper. My voice is weak. Barely audible. I can almost see the syllables rise from my mouth and ascend through the fissure above me.

"Nate? Thank fucking god, man."

Oblivion trembles and quakes as the crack in the nothingness widens. A monstrous wail fills the void once more. I hear the snapping of great jaws. A noise like claws against stone sends tremors through my soul.

I call out to Sebastian again, but my voice won't go above a whisper. It still manages to rise and float through the break in the void

"Save your strength, dude. I'm right here."

I feel a gentle squeeze on my shoulder. Sebastian's hand is

warm and comforting.

The blackness at the edges of the fissure begins to crumble. Falling shards of oblivion ignite with light and mass. They float down around me, like ash and ember after a forest fire. To witness bits of nothing, destroyed by the touch of something—what an odd and beautiful sight.

The serpent snaps at me, urging me deeper into the black. I ignore it and open my eyes. The light hurts. I wince and bring a hand up over my face.

"Here," Sebastian says, taking off his sunglasses and placing them on my face. "You've been out for weeks. No surprise your eyes are so sensitive."

I glance around the room and find that I'm in a hospital bed. Cables are stuck to my skin and tubes stab into my flesh. Machines and monitors beep, click, and whir in a rhythmic tune.

Beep Beep Beep Beep

Pssshhhh woo click click

"What the hell happened to me?"

"You got hammered and wrecked your car."

"Did I hurt anyone?"

"Just yourself. No other cars were involved. Kind of a miracle they found your ass in the middle of the night and the middle of nowhere."

I try to sit up, but I'm too weak. Sebastian pats me on the shoulder and urges me to stay down. I lean my head back against the pillow of my hospital bed and tap along with the music of the medical machinery.

"Not that I don't appreciate it, but what are you doing here, man?" I ask. "We're a long way from California."

"I figured with Dalia and Cleo … you know … " He trails off. Sebastian was never good with expressing his feelings outside of music. "They said you might not make it, but I didn't want you to wake up alone if you did."

"Thank you."

"Whatever, man. Don't get all faggy about it." He says this while resting his hand on mine.

My other hand brushes against something soft. I grasp and hold it up. It's a stuffed crocodile, and as small as it is, my hand still trembles holding it.

"What's this?" I ask

Sebastian shrugs his shoulders.

I examine the toy. It's made from green felt and a seam along the stomach has been ripped open. Tufts of white fluff jut out of its split belly. Bits of stray stuffing stick to its neck, like a mane.

I stick my hand into the stuffed crocodile's wound. The inside of its stomach is cold, unnaturally so. A voice hisses in my ear, telling me to embrace the cold—urging me back into the belly of nothingness.

"I should get a nurse in here, dude. They'll probably wanna take a look at you."

"Not yet. You have your phone, right? Play some music first."

"What do you wanna hear?"

"Something new," I say, tossing the stuffed crocodile aside. "I'd like to hear something new."

July

An old pickup with West Virginia plates speeds by me. The thing looks like it's made entirely out of rust and Bondo. It kicks dust up into the mountain air, covering my jeans with even more dirt. I'm pretty sure they were blue at one point, but now they look the khaki color of those overalls that carpenters wear. I don't mind so much, and I don't think anyone in the bar up ahead is going to care either.

It's hot out and I've been walking forever. I almost regret not buying a new car, but I think hoofing it has been good for me. These old muscles need to move after several weeks in a coma. Let's call it physical therapy.

The sun's on its way down now, and luckily so is the temperature. The water in my bottle is warm, at best, but at least I have water, right? I'll be able to get something colder soon enough.

The bar up ahead is an old mountain roadhouse. Ancient neon signs with outdated logos light up the windows and the decals on the door are bleached white from decades of sunlight. It's the kind of place where people go for their first legal drink and keep going back until their last.

There's a sandwich board out front with the words *Open Mic* scrawled across it in black marker. From inside, I hear a feminine voice and the high register notes of a ukelele.

The inside of the bar is what I expected. Old timers, who probably aren't nearly as old as they look, watching a game at the bar. Young bucks playing darts and acting the fool for pretty young girls. Time moves on, but some things never change.

There's a small stage at the far end of the building. The girl playing the ukelele is young and she has a beautiful voice. She's a bit heavy, and not very pretty, but the song she plays is moving.

I can see the dreaminess and ambition in her eyes. She wants a ticket out of this town, and she thinks this is it. Rock stardom doesn't happen for girls who look like that, however, no matter how talented they are. It makes me angry at all the superficial bullshit that the music industry heaps on artists. It makes me feel embarrassed for being part of that whole dog and pony show for so long.

I wonder how many folks there are out there like that—people with way more talent than Sebastian or I, but who don't look good in a music video. There's no point in dwelling on it, I suppose. The world is how it is, the good and the bad. We can only change what we can change.

Enjoying the ukelele girl's song, I step up to the bar. A tattooed snake slithers up from the bartender's cleavage and coils around her throat. Her blue irises, bisected by a reptilian pupil, regard me coolly.

Her nose, her lips ... they look so much like my Cleo's.

She pours a whiskey and slides it toward me. She smiles, but there is no warmth in it.

"Just water, thanks."

She nudges the whiskey closer toward me. I shake my head and slide it back, then turn toward the stage. I hear an angry hiss, but ignore it in favor of the music playing.

The ukelele girl finishes her set and is met with too little applause. I make my way over to her to let her know how much I enjoyed it, then quickly excuse myself before she thinks I'm some old creep trying to get down her pants.

A few more folks perform. A middle-aged guy plays a Stones song on an acoustic guitar. A young kid dressed in all Carhart gear tells a few jokes. Some burly good old boy recites a bad love poem for his girlfriend. He's met with teasing from his buddies and a kiss from his lady.

My turn to play comes around. I lay my guitar case on the ground and pull out a hollow body Gretsch that Sebastian gave me. My Les Paul got totaled with my Lincoln. I miss it, but it feels kind of nice to be playing something new.

"Evening. My name's Nathan Pharaoh. Some of you older folks might know me, or maybe you don't. Either way, I'd like to play a new song tonight."

I strum an E minor chord and gaze over toward the bar. The bartender looks at me, cold anger carved into her face.

I'm sorry that I wasn't there when you were captive of your fear
I'm sorry that my rambling ways brought us all such despair

The song is slower and softer than the stuff I used to write. It has '50s or early '60s vibe. There's a simplicity to the melody that seems more honest than nearly anything I've ever written before.

And you made the choices that you did, you ripped my soul apart
But it was my own selfishness, that allowed the end to start

I can see her trembling behind the bar. Her serpentine tattoo writhes in anger across her chest. Tears well in her reptilian eyes.

Cleopatra, I love you.
Cleo, I forgive you

Couch Surfing Through the 12 Chambers of Hell

I give the bartender one last glance as I sing the chorus, then shut my eyes. Burning tears leak through my closed lids. When I open them back up, the bartender is gone. The only snake to be seen is on a flag by the door above the words *Don't Tread on Me.*

AUGUST

The sun ascends over the Atlantic. I'm greeted by a slate horizon tinted with orange and gold highlights. The beauty of the fiery sunlight against the cold gray speaks to me like a promise from the gods. There's still more life to live. Still more beauty to see. Still more I can give back to the world.

I light up a cigarette and inhale the smoke, letting it sit in my lungs. I think this is going to be my last one, so I savor it. There are worse places to say goodbye to something you love than on a beach.

I stand at the edge of the sea, the water lapping at my ankles and hermit crabs scrambling around my bare feet. The sun rises higher over the ocean, casting golden light over rocks, seaweed, and beached jellyfish. I find myself pondering life and death. The way those jellyfish will feed the seagulls and the gulls will fall from the sky one day and feed some other scavenger. Nothing truly ends.

I think about my journey across Route 50, and how intent I was on dying. I so badly wanted to join Dalia and Cleo on the other side. Part of me still does. But now I think about all the moments we had, the three of us, and how those are kept alive in my heart and my mind, and how I might commit them to song so they live beyond me as well.

Couch Surfing Through the 12 Chambers of Hell

I thank whatever gods may be for the time I had with my girls. I thank Dalia and Cleo for all the ways they made me a better man, and how their influence can still resonate and make the world a better place if I let it. If I can find the courage to open up and share that with others. If I can be brave enough to live again.

The are tracks in the sand—the zig-zag trails of a serpent. They lead to a mass of rocks, covered in algae and seaweed—into black, hidden places. The serpent still ushers me into that darkness, but its hiss is soft now, barely audible beneath the crashing of golden-capped waves.

About the Author

CURTIS M. LAWSON is a writer, poet, comic creator, editor, and musician. His published works include *Devil's Night, Black Heart Boys' Choir, The Coffin Maker's Book of Dark Tales*, and *The Envious Nothing*. He has also contributed to the writing and development of the TTRPG *Astro Inferno* from Haxan Studios. A key fixture at Weird House Press, Curtis serves as an editor, marketing director, and oversees the Gallows Whisper imprint.

Curtis resides on the outskirts of Providence, RI. In his free time, he pursues his passions of fitness and martial arts and records heavy music under the moniker IX of Blades.

www.ingramcontent.com/pod-product-compliance
Lightning Source LLC
Chambersburg PA
CBHW022042170626
46808CB00003B/1329